# The Bully of Barkham Street

# The Bully of Barkham Street

## Mary Stolz

*Pictures by Leonard Shortall*

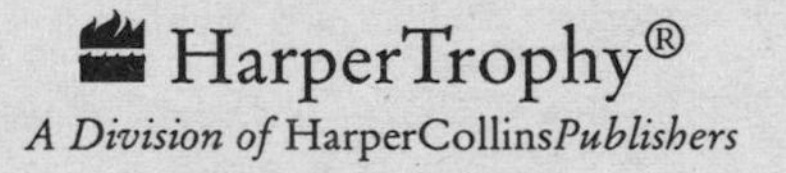

HarperTrophy®
*A Division of* HarperCollins*Publishers*

THE BULLY OF BARKHAM STREET

 Printed in the United States of America.
For information address HarperCollins Children's Books, a division of HarperCollins Publishers, 10 East 53rd Street, New York, NY 10022.

Library of Congress Catalog Card Number: 63-9090
ISBN 0-06-025820-9
ISBN 0-06-025821-7 (lib. bdg.)
ISBN 0-06-440159-6 (pbk.)

First Harper Trophy edition, 1985.

*For Maude Weaver*

# PART ONE

# CHAPTER 1

Martin Hastings wriggled at his desk. He squirmed and yawned and wished the bell would ring. It was the last period of the day, a hazy, hot fall day, and he was restless. Mr. Foran, at the front of the room, went on and on, but Martin paid no attention.

If there was one thing he didn't like (and there wasn't one, there were lots), one thing he absolutely couldn't stand, that thing was school. In the first place his birthday had come in such a way that he had started practically a year later than most kids. Now he'd gone and had what their doctor called "an unusually fine growth spurt." This meant he was bigger than anyone else in his class, which was all right for knocking people down but still made him feel peculiar. He'd taken to sort of hunching around, and his mother was forever saying, "Martin, stand *up*. Don't slouch that way."

He stared out the window, pretending that an invader from space was creeping up the wall, about to swarm into the classroom and disintegrate everyone in it with his nuclear-electronic eye. No one knew except the one boy, Martin Hastings, that DOOM was crawling toward them, handhold, foothold, up and up the side of the wall, scaling it the way a fly would. . . .

The ghastly fingered hands wriggled their way over the sill, the head lifted into view, flat and weavy like a cobra's—

Martin made a horrible face, stretching his lips away from his teeth. He lifted his hands and spread them in air, a creature about to spring upon the enemy! He would sacrifice himself!

*Martin Hastings moved like a whiplash. Fearless, terrifying, his aspect drove the demon backward, away from the window, to a splashing, crashing, bloody death on the cement playground below—*

"Whaaah!" Martin yelled, fiercely, ringingly, in a tone to drive a demon to his death and save the class from utter—

"Martin Hastings!" Mr. Foran shouted. He looked pretty shaken. Briefly Martin thought that if Mr. Foran had been the demon, he'd sure be lying in a puddle of blood in the playground now.

"Martin, will you explain what you think you're doing, yelling that way in the middle of a period?"

"It isn't the middle, it's practically the end," Martin said. He was, of course, just stating a fact. How the fact sounded didn't occur to him until he heard himself stating it.

The class was in an uproar. Boys laughing, girls squealing, Mr. Foran flushed with annoyance.

Oh, *crimers*, Martin said to himself. Now what have I done?

The dismissal bell rang at last, and the class surged to its collective feet, anxious to be gone. Over the hubbub, Mr. Foran said, "Martin Hastings, you will remain at your seat, please."

Martin groaned, dropped back in his chair, and stared at the ceiling. Some of the other kids looked at him and snickered.

"Fourth time this week, isn't it, Marty?" said Jeb McCrae.

"If you count Monday," Martin said with a shrug.

"Oh, let's count Monday. It'd feel so left out if we didn't."

"Funny, funny man," Martin sneered. "It just so happens that on Monday I—"

But Jeb was gone, not waiting to hear. Martin shrugged again, in case anyone was looking, and went on explaining to himself that you couldn't really count Monday, because that day he'd stayed on purpose, trying to find out from Mr. Foran what the arithmetic was all about. Fractions were mysterious and elusive to Martin. He sometimes thought they were just as mysterious and elusive to Mr. Foran, who certainly didn't explain them very clearly.

So Monday didn't count. He'd stayed on purpose, learned nothing, and that had been that.

The other three days—

Well, Tuesday he'd been kept in for holding his thumb over the water spigot of the drinking fountain in the hallway. Thursday it had been for running in the corridors. (He'd had the absolutely Martin-type luck to bowl right into the principal as he rounded a corner.) Today? He cast his mind back to nine o'clock, tried to turn up something he might have done earlier that would seem sufficient to make Mr. Foran keep him in on a Friday. Mr. Foran was for beating it, but fast, on Friday afternoon. There didn't seem to be anything but that sudden shout. What the heck, Martin thought, feeling queasy. What's a little yell at the end of the day? He ought to be grateful, in a way. It woke everybody up, didn't it?

"Martin, will you kindly come up here to my desk?"

Mr. Foran's voice echoed in the empty room, and Martin started nervously. He hadn't noticed that everyone was gone, and probably Mr. Foran had been sitting up there waiting for him to notice for quite a while.

Shoving himself to his feet, Martin sauntered down between the rows of desks. His heart was pounding hard, but Mr. Foran couldn't see that. All he could see was Martin, taking his time.

"Martin," the teacher said in a firm, annoyed voice, "you may have all afternoon to waste, but I do not."

So? said Martin to himself. Who cares? But he moved a little faster and pulled up at the desk, looking in Mr. Foran's eyes with an expression in his own that he knew got grown-ups furious. It was a combination stare, first humble, then bold, that they didn't know how to take. He said nothing.

Mr. Foran's jaw flexed. He waved his hand

toward a paper on the desk top. It was, Martin saw, the assignment that he had somehow managed to get in today, on time. Mr. Foran picked it up, holding it so Martin could see better.

"Well?" he said at length, when Martin remained silent.

"Well, what?"

Mr. Foran dropped—just about threw—the paper to his desk. "Martin, do you deliberately assume that tone of voice, or are you unaware of its effect?"

"What tone?"

"I believe you know."

"No, I don't."

Mr. Foran looked around the room, stretched his neck, fixed his eyes again on the boy. "Do you customarily reply to adults in this fashion?"

You'd think after two months he'd know, Martin said to himself. Aloud he said, "What fashion?"

"Martin, will you stop parroting me?"

"But I don't know what you're talking about."

Martin noted with satisfaction that they were rapidly getting away from the subject of his paper. This was what nearly always happened when grown-ups had "little talks" with him. They started out talking about one thing and ended up in all sorts of other directions and usually mad as heck.

He waited.

"Well?" Mr. Foran said again.

"Well, what?"

"Martin!" The teacher started to his feet, sat down again, drew a deep breath, and said, "At your house, do you never use proper nouns? Do you never say *Yes, Mother* or *What is it, Dad?*"

Martin blinked and let his mouth fall open slightly. This was his dumb look, and almost as distracting to adults as the other one.

"Look here, Martin," Mr. Foran said wearily, "it is more mannerly to say *Yes, Mr. Foran* or *Yes, sir* than just *Yes* or *Well* or *What*. Do you understand?"

"I suppose so."

"You suppose so, *what?*"

"Huh? Oh, well, I suppose . . . I suppose so, Mr. *Foran*. Okay?"

For a second it seemed that the teacher would wave him away, but then, with a funny little snort, he grabbed the paper again and thrust it before Martin's eyes.

"Are you proud of this piece of work?"

Martin looked, as well as he could with the thing two inches from his nose. It was sort of blotty, he guessed. Was that why the old boy was having catnips?

"I got it in in time, didn't I?" he offered, not hopefully.

"And you feel that satisfies the requirements?"

Martin rather thought it had. At the same time— "Doesn't it say good things? I mean, isn't it all right?" As a matter of fact Martin had been a bit proud of the paper. It was a nice imaginative account of a fight between a buffalo and a sea lion, with some tough conversation between the two that had seemed to him just the sort of thing creatures would say to each other in battle times. It had ended with the sea lion pulling the buffalo into the ocean and drowning him. It was a paper for Mr. Foran's "creative writing" class.

"Isn't it creative enough?" he asked, and added, "I mean, Mr. Foran?"

"Martin, this paper is so full of misspellings that it's almost as if you'd gone out of your way to achieve them. And it is quite the sloppiest piece of work handed in to me this year, and that includes other papers by you."

"Yeah, but what about the fight? That was pretty good, wasn't it?"

"That's beside the point."

This seemed to Martin monstrously unfair. He opened his mouth to say so, just as Mr. Foran said, "Yes, yes. The fight was excellent. I'm not questioning your imagination. Far from it. I'm saying that you're sloppy and careless. Also rude," he muttered, "but perhaps that's beside the point just now, too."

Martin scowled and said something under his breath that Mr. Foran elected to ignore.

Handing the paper over, the teacher said, "You will take this home and copy it five times over the weekend, correcting all misspelled words. There are to be no blots, erasures, or crossings-out. Do you understand, Martin?"

Stung past endurance, Martin yelled, "I can't do that!"

"What do you mean, you can't?"

"I mean I *can't*. It'd take me all year to copy that five times. I don't write fast at all, and if I had to look up all those words, too, it'd—"

"Not *if*, Martin. There are no ifs involved here. Five times, by Monday."

"Well, I can't do it, that's all. And I won't, *see*?"

"Ten times," Mr. Foran said angrily.

"But—" Martin subsided as the teacher began to say, "Fif—" He grabbed the paper and ran out of the room, his feet noisy on the wooden floor, so that he wouldn't hear if Mr. Foran did holler something else after him.

Out in the school yard, empty except for some guys shooting baskets, he slowed down. His ears were ringing, his breath coming in short gasps, and he was in such a state of rage and frustration that his vision blurred. It was just plain impossible. It had taken him two weeks to do the one page with *all* its blots and misspellings. And you couldn't count thinking up the plot, the fight, because he'd thought that up in a second, practically. Thinking up stories was never any problem for Martin. But *writing*, the actual act of picking up a pen and getting the words down—it was agony, plain agony. Five, no, ten times by Monday? The guy was crazy. Not even Jeb McCrae, the All-American whiz, could do that.

"Boy, you look like a chewed pork chop," said Otto Sonberg, coming past after retrieving the basketball from a far corner. "What'd old Foran do, threaten to tell your parents?"

"Tell them what?" Martin growled.

Otto grinned. "Son, he could tell them practically anything about you and it'd spell trouble."

"Smart guy. You fracture me."

"Ah, come off it, Marty. You know I was kidding. No, but what'd he do, Marty? What the heck was that, anyway? That was some yell you let out. I thought ten girls were going to faint. Something bite you, or something?"

"What's it to you?"

Otto lifted his shoulders. "Nothing, now you ask. I couldn't care less."

"Then why don't you talk less?"

Otto tossed the ball up in the air, caught it, tossed it again, and said as it fell into his waiting hands, "You know something, Marty? You're gonna wind up without any friends, and that's a fact."

"I can do without *friends,*" Martin sneered, wondering as he spoke why he had to be this way. Maybe Otto really was trying to be friendly. Maybe he'd asked about Mr. Foran not to tease or gloat, but just to—well, to be sympathetic or something. But even as one side of his mind considered this possibility, the other said, Friendly, my left hind foot. Friendly like a buzz saw.

"If you're so *friendly* and all that," he said with elaborate indifference, "how come you didn't ask me to your birthday party? Not that I—"

"Look, Marty," Otto interrupted, looking uncomfortable, "that wasn't my fault. It really wasn't.

I wanted to invite you, sort of. But every time I even mention you, my mother sends sparks out of her hair. It was from that, you know, when she was a den mother, and you were in her den. She says she spent the whole year trying to figure out what to feed us and telling you to stop it or go home."

"Stop what?" Martin sniffed.

"That's what I *said* to her, and she said anything you were doing you should have stopped. That was an exaggeration," Otto admitted fairly. "But you gotta admit she did have to send you home just about every other meeting. I mean, who was it broke my father's Exercycle? And we *told* you not to go near it—"

"Boy, I'm never going to hear the end of that stupid Exercycle, am I?"

"It was not a stupid Exercycle until you got your fat paws on it," Otto yelled.

"Ah, go fry an egg," Martin said.

Otto stared at him, then grinned suddenly. "Hey, that's a real funny saying, Marty, old son. You make it up yourself, out of your imagination? I mean, could I have permission to use it sometime, *please*? *Go fry an egg*. That's really comical—"

Martin walked away, Otto's laugh following him,

and then a burst of laughter from the guys playing ball. Not that there was any reason to think they had to be laughing at him.

He plodded up the hill toward home, wondering how he was going to get those five—no, ten—papers done for dopey Mr. Foran. He couldn't, that was all. What did the guy think he was, Popeye? Panting slightly from the uphill climb—it was an unusually hot fall day—and trying to reach a place on his back that was itching, he thought, as he had thought before, that every single thing in the whole world was against him.

Except Rufus.

His heart lifted. Rufus was his dog. He had only had him three weeks, and he had fought and begged and argued for years to get him. (Or, at least, he thought he'd been fighting just for any dog, but when he saw Rufus, he knew it had been that one dog and no other.) His parents had always refused, absolutely. But then one day Mr. Gaylord, who was Mr. Hastings' boss, had said how he had this eight-month-old puppy who was too rambunctious and too big for the city and would Martin like to have him? If it hadn't been Mr. Gaylord asking, Martin was sure he never would have heard anything about it, but it was Mr. Gaylord, so he did, and he promised to reform and behave like a saint, if only they would let him have Rufus. Incredibly, they had.

Martin was wild about Rufus from the very first. They'd told him he had to get up early and come home on time to walk Rufus, who certainly was rambunctious and took a lot of walking. He was to remember to feed him, and keep him out of the dining room, and train him to behave, and never forget him for even a single day, or that would be the end of Rufus. He was also going to have to get better marks at school, be neater, be smarter, be nicer, get along with everybody, and—it seemed to Martin—guarantee never to make another mistake as long as he lived.

He agreed to it all. Of course he'd do those things. Of course he'd train and feed and walk his own dog. Rufus was his friend, his responsibility, his . . . his just about everything. So naturally he'd never forget to come home right after school, never be too sleepy to get up in the morning in time to take care of him. Of course he'd try to get better marks, be smarter, be nicer, get along with everybody.

And he *was* trying. It was not proving as easy as he'd hoped, and he didn't think he was getting much cooperation from other people, who were probably so used to his reputation that they didn't see how he was attempting to live it down.

He was sorry now he'd put his finger on the water spigot and run in the hallways. At least he was sorry he'd got caught. He really was going to have to try even harder. It was too bad about all that fuss with Mr. Foran today, but there was one thing—his parents weren't apt to find out. His parents never went near the school, the way some people did, visiting teachers and like that. And Mr. Foran wasn't the kind of teacher who went out of his way to look the family up and squeal on people. On the other hand he wasn't the sort of teacher you could fool, in a way, and get around, if you promised enough stuff and looked sorry enough. Mr. Foran was tough. He didn't listen to excuses, even real ones. He just piled more work on you.

Martin sighed and tried again to reach that place on his back and thought how he'd never realized until lately the difficulties involved in being good.

A voice that was behind him and then past like a streak said, "Whyn't you get a horse, Fatso?"

# CHAPTER 2

As far back as he could remember, Martin had found Edward Frost a pain and a pest, about as pleasant to put up with as a nail in his shoe. A guy whose parents were forever fussing over him, taking him on picnics and to the zoo, turning up at school for assemblies and Parents' Nights. A guy whose mother ran the P.T.A. and whose father had been seen pitching a ball to him night after night, week after week, until Birdbrain finally learned to get the bat on it. A guy who didn't have a brother, much less a sister, or any troubles at all, so far as Martin could see.

But there was one thing Edward didn't have that he wanted something awful. Something Martin had and Edward didn't. A dog. That was probably why he'd been even more of a nuisance than ever lately. Calling people names and then running home safe.

Martin had always been able to make Edward run, to make him say uncle, to make him cry, even. The times when he managed to make Edward or any other kid cry were in a way that Martin couldn't understand both the best and the most awful times for him. Somehow he would feel, watching the angry tears streak down a face in front of him, sort of relaxed and proud, sort of *that'll-show-them* (even if he didn't exactly know who *them* was). Then, when he'd hardly had time to feel that, he'd begin to get a little shaky, so he'd have to walk away very fast.

Today, hearing that *Fatso*, Martin forgot everything—the heat, his parents, his promises, even, for one furious moment, Rufus. He ceased to be Martin, desperately trying to turn over a new leaf, and became, in a wrathful upsurge, the bully of Barkham Street.

He took out after Edward, who could run fast but not faster than a wild person two years older and stronger, and in minutes he had Edward flat on the ground, pummeling him and pulling his hair.

"Uncle. Say *uncle*," Martin growled through his teeth.

Edward shook his head, as much as he could with his hair clutched in Martin's fist.

"You better, Weird One. I'm warning you," Martin told him.

"No," Edward gasped.

Martin tightened his grasp and shook Edward's head like a mop. "Say uncle!"

"Uncle," Edward choked out at last, and Martin let him go, watching while the smaller boy slapped the dust off his trousers and started away.

Feeling dissatisfied, not properly victorious at all, Martin shouted, "Don't you forget now! When I tell you to say uncle, you say uncle, *pronto!*"

"You fat dumbbell," Edward yelled, beginning to run again now that he was close enough to make it to his house in safety. "You could heat a building with all that hot air!"

"Ah! The trouble with you is you're jealous," Martin shouted. "You can't have a dog because you're such a slob your parents won't let you!"

Edward kept running, and Martin, breathing hard and itching all over, slouched along in a state of tumult.

"You young bully, why don't you pick on some-one your own size?" said a quavery voice.

With a sense of being beset on all sides, Martin

looked up and saw old Mr. Eckman standing on his porch, shaking a white fist. "Somebody ought to tell your parents on you," the old man yelled hoarsely.

"Mind your own business, Prune Face," Martin called up, and got a kick out of the look on old Eckman's countenance, which did, in fact, look sort of like a prune.

Except for his mother and father, there was no adult Martin wouldn't treat with reckless insolence. Even teachers, even the principal, even policemen. Grown-ups filled him with defiance. Always poking their noses into other people's business, thinking just because they were big they could push any kid around. And they always said that about picking on someone your own size, which was pretty dumb of them. The whole point was *winning*, getting somebody angry or scared. How could you do that with a guy your own size? If he pulled off Otto's cap, for instance, and threw it up in a tree, something he often did to Edward's, would Otto run yelling home? He would not. He'd take a poke at Martin, that's what he'd do. And Martin wasn't sure—not exactly sure—just what he, himself, would do then. Maybe poke back. Maybe run? He just wasn't about to find out.

Leaving Mr. Eckman furious, Martin walked along home faster, hoping that his mother hadn't by any chance stopped work early.

He passed Edward Frost's house, next door to his own, looking to see if Edward was hanging around the safety of his yard, ready to yell *Fatso,* or *Plump Pudding,* before diving through the door. There was no sign of him. Probably inside, complaining to his mother, Martin thought scornfully. Edward's mother, of course, would be there. She always was, afternoons, with cookies and stuff for Edward and his friends.

At his house he was relieved to see the garage doors open, the garage itself empty. His father used their old car to drive to the office, and his mother had the newer one out on her job. She sold cosmetics in people's houses, and it kept her pretty busy afternoons. Martin had never minded, or anyway not very much, and it wouldn't have mattered if he had minded, because the Hastings family needed the extra money she made. He hoped that dopey Marietta was out, too, visiting some of her dopey friends.

In the old days, before Rufus, it hadn't bothered him much, coming home to an empty house. Sometimes he played the radio so loud it practically made the walls shiver. Sometimes he poked around in his father's file box, which was forbidden and pretty dull when you got in it. Sometimes he just stamped around from room to room, blowing his bugle and planning how when he grew up he would always have a house to himself. He was never going to get married or have a family, that was for sure. The second he got old enough, he was going to go somewhere far away and have lots of friends and a dog, but no relatives.

But now . . . Oh, now everything was changed and wonderful.

He came in, threw his books on the stairs, ran through the house to the backyard, calling to Rufus. And there was his large puppy, flailing at the end of the run, bounding around in a fenzy of joy at the sight of his friend. Watching, listening to the wild, welcoming barks, Martin could feel his heart actually get bigger inside him. It almost hurt, this greeting that Rufus gave him every day. It almost made him want to cry, except of course that that would be silly.

Still, the fact was he felt that this rough-furred, obstreperous, rough-voiced dog was fonder of him than anyone else had ever been. And he felt the same way toward Rufus. When he thought this, he didn't put it into words. He didn't think, Rufus loves me more than my parents do, and I love him more than I love them. He just *felt* more welcomed and wanted by his dog then he ever had by people. He felt happier with him.

Mr. Hastings had strung a long rope between some trees, and attached to it a chain on a loop, with Rufus's leash at the end. The dog, when Martin was in school, could run quite a distance in either direction.

Rufus hated it.

"Nothing is ever enough," Mrs. Hastings had said one day when Rufus was barking furiously, straining and leaping at the end of the run. "It reminds me of when you were a little boy, Martin. We had the whole backyard fenced in the way it is now, just so you'd have a lot of space to play in and still be safe. But were you satisfied? You were not. You'd plaster yourself against the gate and yell louder than Rufus there."

"I guess," Martin had said in a moment of wisdom, "no place is big enough if you can't get out of it."

"Your sister never yelled when I put her in the yard."

"Maybe she's a natural jailbird," Martin had said under his breath.

His mother probably heard but ignored it. "Well, what are parents to do?" she asked. "People can't be with their children every minute. A boy can't be with his dog all the time, for that matter. And children and dogs have to be protected, don't they? They can't just run loose."

Martin didn't agree. You could teach a child or a dog not to run away or out in the street, couldn't you? But apparently his parents hadn't felt they could teach him. And they wouldn't let him try with Rufus. He'd told them he could train Rufe to stay inside the fence, but just because he'd leaped it once and run off for a while they refused. They just didn't give anyone a chance. And Martin thought he could still remember pressing against that gate, screaming to be set free. But maybe he didn't. Maybe he just thought he remembered, because it seemed such an awful thing to have happened to him. And old Rufus wasn't giving in, either. He carried on something terrible whenever Martin snapped the leash on and walked away leaving Rufus at the end of the long run that wasn't long enough.

But now he forgot all that.

Martin ran to his dog, released him, and they played a rough-and-tumble game all over the yard. Rufus bounding and barking, pretending to bite, but never really biting even a little bit, and Martin happy in a way he had never known except with this dog.

After a long time they sat down together on the grass that was turning brown but still smelled almost summery hot. Martin, rubbing the dog's rough short hair, explained to Rufus that in spite of all his resolutions he still was not a perfect boy.

"It's like this, Rufe," he explained. "I *mean* to be practically Saint Martin, and I can start out pretty good, but then things happen. Like today, that crumb-bun gives me enough homework to keep me going till I'm on Social Security, and he says it has to be done by Monday. Now I ask you, could *you* copy over a whole page of work ten times by Monday and spell everything right?"

Rufus cocked his head consideringly. He let his tongue loll out and a drop dripped from the end of it.

"That's just how I feel about it," Martin said comfortably. "It's an *im*possibility. And then—" He scratched his head, trying to figure out how the fracas with Edward and Mr. Eckman had started.

"Oh, yes—then old Frosty-Wosty next door comes haring by yelling things at me, and what am I supposed to do? Say, *Yes, Eddie old top, you couldn't be righter?* I mean, you can't just let someone call you names, can you?"

Rufus barked and lifted one front paw to Martin.

"Hey," said Martin with delight. "You're learning. Hey, that's a good, good dog—"

Rufus, who always responded madly to praise, let out a series of barks.

Martin and his dog practiced shaking hands, and once Martin looked up and saw Edward Frost, standing in his yard next door, looking wistfully at Rufe.

Seeing that look on Edward's face, knowing what it must feel like to watch another fellow with a splendid dog like Rufus, Martin almost called over the hedge, "Come on and play with him, if you want to."

But he hesitated. A friendly overture toward Edward Frost wasn't a thing he could just rush into. On the other hand, it'd be sort of good to be the one who could give somebody something. It wasn't often Martin found himself in such a position. In fact, he couldn't remember ever being in it before at all. And it wasn't as if Rufus would get to like Edward better, or anything like that. Martin knew that Rufe was his dog, his companion, his friend. Agreeable he might be to other people, but that was just good nature and high spirits. At bottom it was Martin he cared for.

So, Martin went on to himself, this might be a chance to improve his social record a bit. If he started by getting along with Edward Frost, he might end up getting along with everyone in the world. And then his parents would be pleased with him, all right. Well, it was worth a try.

"Come on over," he called to Edward. "You can play with him some. I'm teaching him tricks."

Edward frowned, started forward, stopped, and scowled. "Huh," he said after a moment. "So you can sic him on me? Fat chance, Fat Boy."

The old familiar rage flashed through Martin, dissipating his impulse toward friendliness. He scrambled to his feet and faced Edward, who backed away. Rufus decided they were going to play some more. He bounded up happily. Waving his tail in expectation, he waited for the fun to begin.

Just to watch him made Martin smile. He didn't want to. He tried not to. But there was something about Rufus— In a peculiar way he emptied a person of anger.

"Come on, Rufe," he said. "Let's go inside."

Without looking again at Edward, Martin and his dog went into the house. Martin made himself a sandwich, gave Rufus half, ate some cake left over from the night before, and went up to his room, where he blew on his bugle, forgetting all about the assignment for Mr. Foran.

He was playing so loud that he didn't hear his mother come in and up the stairs. All of a sudden, there she was at his door.

"Martin," she said sternly, "what's that dog doing on your bed?"

Martin dropped his bugle, retrieved it, stared at Rufus, who'd been curled up comfortably on the spread but was now sneaking to the floor with his tail drooping.

"Gee, he must've got up there, Mom. Just this very second, I mean. He—I mean, we—know he's supposed to stay on the floor. I mean—"

"Martin, you've been warned about him. Don't ever say you haven't."

Martin felt a chill in his blood. "What do you mean, Mom?" he asked nervously.

"Just what I say. You've been warned. And don't

think you can come home late and get away with it just because I'm not here."

"I didn't—" Martin began, and then thought better of it. It wasn't that he minded lying. He lied quite a lot. Only not when he clearly couldn't get away with it. "How do you know I was late?" he said instead.

"Never mind how I know."

"Marietta told you, didn't she?" he said furiously. He thought he had seen his sister, far down the street in a gaggle of girls, when he'd been trudging up the hill toward home. What terrible luck that she'd seen him, too. Boy, what a sister. He only just kept himself from saying something poisonous about her, a move sure to get him in even more hot water.

"What I came up to find out," Mrs. Hastings went on, "is what happened to all my freezer tape?"

"Your freezer tape," said Martin, trying not to look in the direction of his model airplane.

"Yes, Martin. My freezer tape. I'm going to make chili con carne tonight, to freeze. And now I find that the tape is gone. There was some there last week. So where is it now?"

Martin took a deep breath. In spite of himself,

his eyes went to the table where the airplane model stood. He'd borrowed the freezer tape a few days before to use on the airplane and had forgotten to tell his mother. Again. One way or another, "borrowing" was getting him in a lot of trouble. Within recent weeks he'd lost his pen, borrowed Marietta's and lost it, gotten talked to very hard by his father, then borrowed his mother's pen and lost that, too. That time his father had whacked him.

His mother walked over to the table, studied the airplane model, picked up the bit of smudged and gluey tape that was left, dropped it, and turned to Martin.

"You know," she said, "this practically amounts to dishonesty, this process that you call borrowing."

"Well, gee. I didn't think the old tape was that important. I *needed* it, and you weren't here, and —well, what was I supposed to do?"

"I can think of several alternatives. Go out and buy your own. Use something else. Do without. Or at the very least *tell* me that you've taken it and that there isn't any left for freezing purposes. Now, I'd like you to go to the store, please."

"Oh, sure," he said eagerly. "Sure thing."

"Here's the list, and here's money for the other

things. For the freezer tape, please use your own."

"But I don't have any," Martin wailed.

"Then use what's there, and we'll take it out of your allowance next week."

"But that isn't—" Martin began, and subsided quickly. He supposed, awful as it was, that what his mother asked *was* fair. In spite of this decision, he stamped out angrily to get his bike. He had to clip Rufus back to the run, because his parents didn't want the dog tearing along beside him while he biked. They said it was dangerous. Martin knew it was not, but the thing about adults—the thing he guessed he held against them the most, and he held a lot against them—was that they didn't have to be reasonable or right to get their way, they just had to be grown up.

Just wait till I am, Martin said to himself, pedaling toward the A & P. Just wait. He made a face, thinking about it. He hated the whole idea of being a grown-up. They had such dull lives all of them, such dumb ways of looking at things. He didn't really think he'd be like that, but on the other hand, who could tell what happened to a guy when he grew up? Maybe your whole self changed. Hard to believe, but still—there they all were, all the same, and all impossible.

Somehow he lost the list on the way to market and had to telephone his mother to find out what he was buying, which annoyed her. Then when he got home and took Rufus up to his room, Rufus tried to get back on the bed and had to be scolded, which depressed Martin. Finally he settled at his desk and began the dreadful task of copying.

When three copies had been blotted, and he hadn't even been able to find in the dictionary half the words he'd misspelled (how could you look up a word if you couldn't spell it?), he was ready to bellow. Just as he crumpled the third try, the doorbell rang, and when his mother answered Mrs. Frost said, loud enough to scare a ghost, "I am here, Mrs. Hastings, to find out if you intend to do anything about that son of yours?"

Oh, *crums*, Martin thought. I guess I'll run away.

"Precisely what do you mean by that?" Mrs. Hastings said, keeping Mrs. Frost standing on the porch.

"I mean precisely what I say, what are you going to do about that—that juvenile delinquent you're rearing?" Mrs. Frost, usually pretty easygoing, sounded close to tears, she was so mad. Martin listened, almost too interested to go on being nervous. That was *no* way to go about complaining to his mother. Offhand, he couldn't think of any way that would work.

"You watch what you're saying, Mrs. Frost," said Mrs. Hastings. "What makes you think you can go around accusing—"

"I don't think," Mrs. Frost said shrilly. "I'm *telling* you. It's getting so my son is afraid to come home from school. Do you know, he tells me that every day, every single day, when he starts out of the school building, he says to himself over and over, *Let him not be there, let Martin not be there.* How would you like one of your children to feel that way?"

"Your boy's a tease. He's probably asking for it. I've heard him call Martin all sorts of names and then run in the house like a coward."

"Don't you call my child a coward. He's smaller and younger than Martin, who's built like a—" Mrs. Frost broke off.

"Yes?" Mrs. Hastings prodded coldly. "You were saying?"

"Nothing," Mrs. Frost said, sounding tired. "I'm not going to call a child names. Martin's a child, even if he does sometimes behave like a devil. I'm simply asking what you intend to do about it. He's a rude, bullying boy. He's disrespectful even to a poor old man like Mr. Eckman—"

"Mr. Eckman is an old snoop."

"He saw that roughneck sneak up on Edward and knock him down from behind. I'd scarcely call that snooping."

"I told you, Edward was probably asking for it."

"Let me tell you, Mrs. Hastings, you're asking for something yourself."

"Are you threatening me?"

"I'm telling you," Mrs. Frost said again.

Martin, in the upstairs hall, listening to all this, had a sense of crazy glee. Two grown women fighting like that, and all because of him. For the moment, while it lasted, he couldn't even care much that as soon as Mrs. Frost left his mother would light into him, but good.

Well, there was one thing sure. If you couldn't get them to listen to you when things were all right, you sure caught their attention when trouble was stirring.

Suddenly the front door closed with a bang, and Mrs. Hastings' voice came up the stairs. "Martin! Martin Hastings, come down here this instant."

All bliss departed as Martin crept down to his punishment.

He caught it from his mother. Then, when his father came home, he caught it all over again. He tried to take comfort from the fact that no matter how angry they got with him they never listened to anybody else who was angry with him. Martin couldn't count the times that people had come storming up to the door to complain about his behavior. Or telephoned, yelling so you could hear them across the room. They never seemed to make any impression at all.

Somehow this knowledge didn't comfort him. Because, though he couldn't exactly explain it, it seemed to him his parents weren't really defending Martin, their son. It seemed to him they were just refusing to give the neighbors any satisfaction. His parents didn't like other people telling them off.

After a long, loud lecture and couple of hard smacks on the bottom, Martin was sent to his room by Mr. Hastings. As he got to the living room door his father said, "Oh, and one other thing, Martin."

Sluggishly, filled with a hot, mean sensation that he tried not to let show, Martin turned.

"You've been sufficiently warned about that dog, Martin. If I come home to one more evening like this, that's the end of Rufus, understand? You were allowed to have the dog on condition that you behave yourself in every respect. That's your final warning."

Overwhelmed, Martin went to his room.

Behave himself in absolutely every respect. How could he do that? How could anybody do it? If you had a tattletale sister, guys who teased, teachers who were unfair, parents who wouldn't listen to you, how could you behave yourself in practically any respect? Why, just about anything he did could look like misbehavior, whether it was or not. He was supposed to *let* people make fun of him? He was supposed to act like an angel, get home on the dot every day? How could he get home on the dot if Mr. Foran didn't let him out on it?

Burning tears streaked down his face as he contemplated the three crumpled papers on the floor and wondered how he was ever going to get one, much less ten, decent copies done by Monday.

Everywhere he looked, everything he thought about, just was more trouble. Borrowing, lying, getting into fights, failing subjects.

And in all this there was only Rufus.

Martin sat down now and put his arms around the thick, shaggy neck of his dog. He didn't say anything, and Rufus remained very still, as if he understood. Only the long fringy tail moved, gently, from side to side.

# CHAPTER 3

A week later Martin had done two perfect copies of the paper and now had twenty-eight to go. Every day when Mr. Foran found out he hadn't done the number he was supposed to have done already, he added some more.

It was all, so far as Martin was concerned, completely crazy. He wasn't even attempting to catch up any more. He was kept so busy trying to behave in other ways, ignoring Edward Frost, apologizing to Mr. Eckman, walking and talking sedately, trying not to interrupt or yawn in class, that the papers, especially now that they'd reached such an astronomical figure, hardly seemed important. He worked at them some each night, and each day was given more to work at.

At least Mr. Foran wasn't keeping him in any more. Or, anyway, he hadn't until yesterday, when he'd tacked on half an hour for what he called talking back and Martin called explaining. But Martin had run all the way home and had gotten there before Marietta or his mother. He was ready to swear that Marietta, this time, didn't know he'd been late.

He was thinking about this as he walked home, on time today, fast but not running. There was something about a fat boy running that brought out the sniper in other guys. Yesterday he'd had a terrible struggle with himself to keep from belting Rod Graham, a friend of Edward's and just as much of a pest.

"Go it, Blimpo . . . go, go," Rod had called across the street. "Go, go, Blimpo-po."

For the sake of Rufus, Martin had ground his teeth together and kept running. Today, not being late, he was just walking briskly, contemplating his troubles.

He decided he was going to get started on those papers and not stop till every one was done. This was Friday. He'd work all weekend, not stopping to eat or sleep.

"I'll show them," he muttered to himself. "I'll show all of them."

Maybe if he went without sleep or food and

worked until the pen fell from his fingers and he himself fell to the floor in a state of exhaustion, then maybe Mr. Foran and his parents and all would see what a hard worker he was. Maybe then they'd feel sorry for him.

He wondered if he could work hard enough to make himself so sick that he'd die. He could see their faces, pale and worried, hovering over his bed.

"Do you see what you've done?" his father would be shouting at Mr. Foran. "You've driven this boy to the *grave* with your cruel injustice." Mr. Foran would be a wreck, trembling, wringing his hands. "I'm sorry, I'm so sorry . . . oh, if I had only known . . . if I had only known." Martin saw himself, lying there weak and beyond human aid. He could feel the strength leaving his limbs, the breath leaving his body. He felt it so much that he almost stopped walking. He would open his eyes heavily, lift one pale limp hand and say, "It was nobody's fault. I blame no one." Then his mother would fling herself at the bedside, crying, "Oh, Martin, Martin . . . speak to me. . . . How brave and good you are, my son. And we didn't know, we never knew. . . . Martin, *speak to me*. . . ." But, with a little smile for Rufus, he would turn his face to the wall and die with that one little word unsaid—

There was something awfully familiar about this, Martin realized, walking a little faster. Besides the fact that he'd gone through it in various versions many times before. Now where— Oh, yes. Tom Sawyer. And probably plenty of other guys, too. It seemed a shame to Martin that boys apparently had to about die to get some kindness and attention, where girls could get it just by—by whining and being girls. Or did he mean just boys like himself and Tom Sawyer? Otto, Edward Frost, Jeb McCrae, fellows like that, they seemed to get plenty of T.L.C. from their families. Teachers liked them. They had all these friends.

So what? Martin said to himself. So just what? Would he rather be like them or like old Tom Sawyer, in trouble the whole time with the whole world? It crossed his mind that Tom, in spite of all his fights, had had some best friends. Martin didn't have a best friend. He sort of got along with some of the guys, Otto, Jeb, a few others, some of the time. But he couldn't even say he had friends, let alone best ones.

How did a person get in a position where he didn't have any friends?

A couple of times, when he'd been younger, Martin had been asked to join clubs, secret societies. One had folded after a week, because they had so many arguments over who was to be president. The other one he'd been kicked out of because—so they said—he talked so much nobody else ever got a chance. He'd had all that trouble in the Cub Scouts mostly because Otto's mother didn't like him. She said he was noisy and a nuisance. She said he broke that Exercycle. It had just been ready to break when he got on it, but since he'd been told not to get on it at all, he hadn't been able to defend himself. Sometimes Martin thought he was the unluckiest person who'd ever lived.

Now he shrugged and said to himself, So what?

He didn't care if he had a best or any friends. He didn't care if people liked him or not. There weren't fellows like Huck and Jim that you could be friends with any more anyway. The whole world of Tom Sawyer was gone. You could feel like him, wild and tough and barefoot. You could feel like Huckleberry Finn himself, abandoned and on his own. But feeling like them and being like them were different matters. Martin knew he'd be scared to death alone in a fog on a raft in the Mississippi. He didn't want to be abandoned and on his own.

He mounted the porch steps, those papers for Mr. Foran heavy on his mind and somehow no longer a challenge. He'd never in the world be able to do it. Not if he lived to be as old as Prune Face Eckman. He'd never get twenty-eight, or even five copies done, and probably by this time next week it'd be up to seventy-five. And he wouldn't go without food or sleep because he was already starving, and when night came he'd get sleepy even if he doused his head with ice water. He knew, because he tried sometimes staying up all night and had never managed it even once.

"I hate this town and that school and . . . and everything," he muttered, going into the empty house. But then, of course, he remembered Rufus, and then he couldn't go on hating anything.

Tossing his books on the stairs, he ran through the kitchen, threw open the back door and called, "Hey, Rufe! Here I am!"

The backyard was empty, quiet. The lead hung from the runway, trailing limply over the grass.

"That's funny," Martin grumbled to himself, refusing to be scared. "That's very funny."

He went back into the house to see if by any

chance his mother had left Rufus inside, knowing all the while that it was impossible. Rufus would have bounded into sight at the first sound of Martin's arrival. Unless . . . maybe he was sick somewhere, lying alone, unable to bark?

Martin looked everywhere. Basement, attic, his own room, even Marietta's and his parents. Not in the house. No Rufus.

Perhaps, he thought, old Rufe has finally managed to break away from the leash? Perhaps he's running around the neighborhood at this very minute, free as a bee, having a real wingding? Reassuring himself in this manner, Martin yet felt his heart shriveling into a cold little lump, felt the stirrings of panic in his veins.

He went back to the yard to examine the run. The leash was not broken, not wrenched away. It lay there, useless but quite intact. Somebody had taken his dog off the run. There wasn't any other answer. Only why? Had his mother decided to take Rufus along in her car today, for company maybe? Martin knew perfectly well she had not. His mother kept that car as neat and shining as her own room, and Rufus had about as much chance of riding in it as he had of sleeping every night on a bed—which was no chance at all.

Had some darn kid from the neighborhood—Edward, maybe—let Rufus loose, just out of spite?

Maybe Rufe had got sick and his mother had taken him to the vet. Except that this morning the dog had been as healthy as a—as a horse.

All the while he stabbed around in this direction and that, looking for possible explanations, the truth was circling the edges of Martin's mind like a hornet.

Rufus was gone.

He was gone, and forever. Somehow Martin hadn't been good enough, hadn't lived up to what his parents called "his side of the bargain," and he wasn't ever going to see his dog again.

What had he done wrong?

He was told, in the very beginning, about all the things he'd have to do in order to keep Rufus. Get up early and walk him. Well, he had, just about every day. Once or twice on a weekend, when it had been so rainy and gray he hadn't thought anybody, even Rufus, would want to go out and walk, he'd just sort of kept on sleeping and his father had taken the dog out of the house to fasten him to the run.

He'd been kept in by Mr. Foran a pretty good lot of times, but he'd always gotten home before anybody else and in plenty of time to walk and play with Rufus. Except that afternoon Otto and Jeb had asked him to play touch football. Even knowing that it was only because they didn't feel they had enough fellows, Martin had still been so pleased that he forgot all about going home until he was late for dinner. So nobody was fooled that day. And it was too hard to explain. How could you tell your parents that touch football wasn't a thing that happened to you every day? You'd sound like a dope, explaining how it felt like such an honor you forgot even your dog. And if he *had* felt able to explain just to his parents—he might have—it was absolutely out of the question with Marietta sitting there, watching. So he'd just said, in a casual way, as if it were a thing he did all the time, "I stopped to play touch football with Otto and the guys." Despite all the probable consequences, he'd felt that stir of pride, saying it.

But on the whole he still thought he'd done fairly well since Rufus came. Only a couple of swipes at Edward, when honor practically demanded it. A little bit of sass to Mr. Eckman, who even Martin's own mother said was a snoop. And then he'd gone and apologized, all on his own. That was about it. He hadn't borrowed anything, or broken or lost anything, in ages. He'd agreed to run errands even when he knew darn well it was Marietta's turn, and he was certainly behaving like Cecil Fancypants in that dumb dancing class they forced him to go to. Bowing to the girls, ma'aming Miss Troy, the dancing mistress, keeping his white gloves on all evening, and dancing every dance.

*What did they want?* How good and perfect did somebody have to be to keep—to keep—

He folded his lips tight together and wound the leash tight in his fists, trying to rip it apart. Then he put it between his teeth and bit down until his jaws hurt.

I hate them, I hate them, I hate them, he said to himself. They're horrible and unfair and I'm always going to hate them. . . .

They were going to tell him it was his own fault. They'd point out how they had warned him, how they'd told him over and over what would happen if he neglected his responsibility, if he got the family into rows with the neighbors. All that was true, all right. Only something else is true, Martin thought, sitting on the grass with the leash now limp between his fingers. Besides the stuff that he wasn't going to be able to argue about because they *had* warned him was the fact that they'd known all along this would happen. They knew he'd forget sometimes and get into trouble sometimes. So all they'd had to do was wait while he gave them enough excuses so that they could take the dog away and blame it on him.

It seemed to Martin the worst injustice he had ever known of.

He detached the leash from the run, took it up to his room, and then just sat, waiting for his mother to come home. When she did, he got to his feet and clumped down the stairs, following her into the kitchen, where he stood dangling the leash until she turned.

"Well, Martin?" she said at last, sounding tired and dull.

"You took him away, didn't you?"

She drew a deep breath and nodded.

"I hate you," he said slowly, to be sure she'd hear.

Mrs. Hastings closed her eyes briefly, opened them and said, "I'm sure you do." Then, losing that sad and draggy tone, she said suddenly, "What did you expect, Martin? We warned you, and warned you, and warned you. You didn't get one chance, you got fifty. And still you ignored us. Playing ball after school instead of coming home, getting in fights with the neighbors, getting *me* into fights with them. How far do you think you can go? How much do you think you can get away with?"

"You took him away," Martin repeated. It was all he could say.

"That dog has chewed the furniture, ruined Marietta's hat, and a pair of your father's shoes. He's jumped on the living room chairs over and over with his muddy paws. And the neighbors complain that he barks all day while you're away. The simple fact is, Martin, that I cannot manage a job, manage this house, and take just about complete care of that dog, too."

"You did not!" Martin cried out, stung and angered. "I took plenty of care of—"

"You attended to him and played with him when it suited you. If a ball game that you preferred came up, so much for the dog."

That darn ball game, Martin thought. That one darn dumb stupid game of touch football that I was too flattered to say no to.

"That game—" he began. If his mother understood, if, at last, he told her how he felt, how he didn't have any friends, maybe she'd be sorry for him, maybe she'd—

The words stuck in his throat. He couldn't, just could not, confess how it was with him. How he was a fat bully who talked too much that nobody wanted on their team or in their club or anything. There were things you just couldn't tell, to anybody.

Only—if he didn't—if he didn't, there was no chance of ever getting Rufus back.

"You see," he began again, "that ball game—"

Marietta came in. She whirled around a couple of times and ended in a pose, with her arms in the air.

"*Guess* what? I am going to play the *lead* in the spring play! *I* am Miranda. . . . *O brave new world,* etc. I want to tell you, Sue Hanberry was but absolutely *dying* to get it, and she thought it was all set for—"

"Marietta, be quiet," Mrs. Hastings said. "Martin and I are having a discussion."

"Ooops," said Marietta. "What's his trouble this time?"

"You pasty pill, you inchworm!" Martin yelled, whirling on her. "Mind your own dumb business, will you?"

"Mama! Don't let him talk to me that—"

"Marietta, will you please go away?" Mrs. Hastings said grimly.

"Go where? Why should I? It's my house, too, isn't it?"

Suddenly Martin burst into tears. He ran stumbling up the stairs and hunched in his chair, crying in jagged, painful gasps, indifferent to Marietta's reaction, to his mother's, to anything in the world but this terrible feeling of loss, a loss they'd say he'd brought on himself and that still still still was not fair.

"Not fair, not fair," he choked, pushing his fists into his eyes until they ached, and he seemed to be looking at a dark red field with lines traveling across it like snakes. "Not fair . . ."

"Martin? Martin, stop crying and look at me, will you?"

Martin sniffled, gulped, dragged a deep breath into his lungs, and stared at his father. "When did you get home?" he said, for lack of anything else to say.

"Just now. Look, Marty, I know how you feel. But the fact is, we warned you repeatedly—"

"Yeah. I know. Mom just gave me the same sermon," Martin said recklessly. "You don't have to go through it again."

"I don't care for your tone, Martin."

I don't care for your tone or you, Martin thought. But he kept quiet this time and just looked through throbbing eyes at his father. Would he turn on his heel and walk out or explain some more about whose fault everything was? Martin waited without interest.

Mr. Hastings sat down on the bed. "Listen to me, Marty. There are things that happen in life that just can't be helped. You're too young and too busy in school to take on the responsibility of a dog, and your mother can't take it for you, and neither can I. I knew this when Mr. Gaylord gave the dog to you, and I took it against my better judgment. But you begged and pleaded so, and promised— Well, the fact is you made promises we should have known you couldn't keep, that were too hard for you. In a way this is our fault as much as it is yours." Mr. Hastings pushed a hand through his hair and added, "Maybe more."

This surprised Martin so much that he couldn't think what to say in answer. He thought it was their fault, too, more than his, but he'd never expected his father to say so. The admission left him sort of stranded, without a place to pin his anger.

"What's going to happen to Rufus?" he said at

last. The name, saying it, made him hurt inside horribly. "Where did she take him?"

His father did not, as he usually did, say, Don't call your mother *she*. If he had, Martin was going to say, Don't call Rufus *it*.

But Mr. Hastings just answered the question. "Mr. Gaylord took him back. Martin, try to be reasonable. Try to think of your dog. He's going to be sent up to Mr. Gaylord's farm, where he'll be darned sight better off than cooped up on a run in our backyard, yelling his lungs out all day. I think it might help if you did try thinking of the dog, instead of yourself."

Easy to say. His father hadn't ever sat with his arms around that shaggy neck, knowing comfort, companionship. His father didn't know what it was like to be—to be—

"Where's the farm?" he asked, swallowing hard.

"Upstate. Mr. Gaylord said you could go visit Rufus sometime."

"Did he?" Martin said dully.

Mr. Hastings got to his feet. "Martin, whether you believe it or not, your mother and I are sorry about this. But you were warned—"

Oh, go fry an egg, Martin said, but just to himself. He wanted to be alone. He wanted to see if knowing Rufus was happy and carefree on a farm would make up for never seeing him again. Or only seeing him at Mr. Gaylord's *sometime*.

When at last he was by himself, Martin put the leash away in the back of his closet, where it would be there but he wouldn't have to look at it. He started trying to think of Rufus happy and independent on a farm instead of thinking about his own life with no Rufus in it. He tried, in other words, to be unselfish and found it even harder than being "good."

He wondered if goodness and unselfishness were something that adults talked about when what they really meant was Don't bother us.

Not, he told himself, that he was going to bother much about goodness any more. What was the point? "*Good,*" he snorted. "Crums to that."

In time he found that you couldn't go on missing a dog, even one you'd loved the way he loved Rufus, every minute of the day. He didn't ever really forget Rufus, but he didn't really always remember him either.

And he didn't go on hating his parents. They were his parents, so he couldn't. Hating them hadn't made him feel better, it had made everything worse. And when he tried to be fair, and he sometimes did try, he saw that maybe they had thought they were being fair. Grown-ups had this strange way of feeling about things. They figured that the less trouble, the better off everyone was. Rufus on a run in their backyard was a trouble. Rufus on a farm was none at all. So to their way of thinking, everyone ought to be pleased, including Martin.

Martin himself kept insisting in his mind that old Rufe was much better off this way. He guessed he even believed it. But it didn't help nearly the way his parents thought it should.

One day, a couple of weeks after that worst day of his life, Martin told Otto about it. He had to tell someone, and Otto was about the only person he could think of who would stop and listen.

"Oh, boy, if that isn't one lousy trick," Otto said in a tone of outrage that warmed Martin's heart. "They just took him away, just like that?"

"Well, they sorta warned me, a few times before," Martin mumbled, not wanting to relinquish his wronged position, but not, either, wanting Otto criticizing his parents. You could criticize them yourself, but other people—

"Want to come home with me?" he heard Otto say. "We could hack around, do something."

"Well, gosh. Sure," said Martin, feeling pleased.

Mrs. Sonberg, when she saw him, looked as if she'd gotten a headache all of a sudden. She said, "Martin, you behave yourself this afternoon, understand?"

This was no way, Martin insisted to himself later in the day, to greet a guest. Even one you thought had broken your husband's Exercycle. He didn't say anything. He gave her one of his looks, that was all.

After they'd played ball for a while, he and Otto sat on the back steps eating some stuff Mrs. Sonberg gave them. Martin tried to talk Otto into playing hookey the next day.

"We can go into St. Louis," he suggested. "On the bus. And we can spend the whole day hacking around. Maybe go to the movies or something," he concluded vaguely, the project being unclear in his mind.

Mrs. Sonberg, who apparently sneaked around listening to people, stormed out on the porch. "Martin Hastings," she said, "I am sick and tired of the way you behave. Now, it is of no importance to me how *you* spend your school days, but—"

Martin found that pretty unfriendly and gave her a look to let her know. For a second she seemed to forget what she'd been saying, then she went on even more angrily. "Now, listen to me, Martin. You are not to come around here any more, trying to—to corrupt Otto. Do you understand?"

"Oh, Mom. For the luva mud, we were joking," Otto said.

"Martin didn't sound as if he meant it as a joke. I happen to know he's played hookey many times."

Now this was unfair. Once, just once, Martin had decided to see what it was like, playing hookey. Kids in books and the movies did it all the time. He'd started hitchhiking to St. Louis and with his usual luck had thumbed an unmarked police car. He'd been carted off to the station house, where the cops had phoned the principal and then his house, getting his mother all steamed up, and everybody in the whole town practically had heard about it.

But that was the only time. And he had been joking just now. Otto knew it. He knew it. But Mrs. Sonberg—

He looked at her and said, "You don't happen to know from beans, see? I only played hookey once, as an experiment, and—"

"Martin, go home. Go home this instant. I will not stand here and be talked back to."

"Whyn't you sit down, then?"

He could not help it. Things like that almost said themselves. It was just like the days of the Cub Scouts. Just about every other week he and Mrs. Sonberg had gotten into one of these hassles, and they'd always ended the same way. *Martin, go home, go home, go home. . . .*

Filled with rage, Martin jumped to his feet, shouting, "You bet your old grandmother's hair-piece I'll go home, and I wouldn't come back here if you paid me!"

"Don't you talk to my mother that way," Otto said, starting forward.

Martin turned, fists up. "Watch your step, Otto-Wotto. I'll pulverize you."

"Yeah? You and how many others?"

"Why, you soda straw—I could mash you with my brains tied behind me."

"So that's where you keep them? I always wondered."

"You two stop!" Mrs. Sonberg shouted. "Otto, go in the house. And you, Martin—"

"I know," Martin mimicked in a high, ladylike voice. "Go home, Martin. Go home!"

So he went home.

Mrs. Sonberg called to talk it over with his

mother. She didn't get very far. Mrs. Hastings said in that cold voice she got with people who were trying to talk Martin over with her that it must have been a misunderstanding, good-bye.

Martin was sent to his room without dinner. He lay on the bed, thinking how in books somebody (usually the mother) always came up with a nice warm supper on a tray for the boy who'd been sent to bed without it by his cruel father.

Well, he didn't get any nice warm supper on a tray.

The next morning Otto said when they arrived at the same time at the school gates, "Wow, that was some wingding, wasn't it?" He didn't ask Martin home again, but the two of them got along pretty well just the same. Probably, Martin had to admit, because Otto just plain got along with everybody.

Gradually things in Martin's life slumped back to normal. He supposed. Normal, for him, meant that he was far from being Saint Martin. He didn't get along with everybody. He practically didn't get along with anybody. Not that he gave a darn.

Only sometimes, coming in after school and finding the house so still and dull and empty, he'd get that feeling of hearing Rufus bark a wild welcome, and he'd remember how the big puppy had leaped against the air, almost strangling to get at his friend, Martin. And then this funny, achy thing would catch at his throat. After a while, if he ate, or blew his bugle, or played the radio, but mostly if he ate, it would go away.

# CHAPTER 4

By the time of the first winter snowfall, Martin had labored out nine copies of the assignment for Mr. Foran. Nine neat (just about neat) copies with correct spellings all the way through. Since Mr. Foran, in a burst of kindness or common sense, had stopped at thirty copies, there were now only twenty-one to go. Martin figured to have the entire punishment finished up by late spring.

Looking out of the classroom window now, he noticed the first large lazy snowflakes spiraling down and let out a yelp of delight.

Mr. Foran frowned, sighed, and said, "What is it this time, Martin? Madmen from Mars, or vanquishers from Venus?"

The class smiled agreeably. They always knew when Mr. Foran had made a little joke, not so much by what he said as by the way he looked.

"It's *snowing!*" Martin told them, unable to repress his joy. A few minutes ago when he'd looked, there'd been nothing out there but gray air and tree branches skinny and bare as steel wires. And now look. Falling thicker by the second, it seemed, came snow. And you could tell by looking that it was dry, powdery snow. Not wet stuff that would melt and just leave everything cold and slimy, but snow that was going to stick. Sledding snow, in other words.

Mr. Foran looked, and it seemed to please him too. He glanced at his watch and said, "I'll tell you what. There are only five minutes of this period left and then morning recess. If you'll get into your things now, you can be ready to shoot out the second the bell rings. Try," he said, lifting his voice as the class shot out of its seats and toward the locker room. "Try not to disintegrate the building with your voices, if it isn't asking too much!"

His request was lost in the uproar, and when the recess bell rang, the sixth grade was out in the yard before the rest of the classes had left their rooms. They ran about yelling, opening their mouths wide to catch the falling icy flakes. There was nothing to do about the snow as yet, since it barely whitened the ground, like a dusting of flour, but oh, the promise of it! With any luck, by the time school let out, they'd be able to form snowballs. With good luck, they'd be obliged to get out their sleds.

Martin stood a little apart, hands in his pockets, watching Jeb and Otto sparring with each other. They belonged to the Y, where they took boxing and other stuff. Martin belonged, too, but never went. When his mother had asked why, he'd said it was because the building wasn't well heated. "I get cold," he'd explained, and since his mother was always worrying about his health, she agreed that it was best for him not to go. Actually, it was because he'd gotten tired of being razzed about his weight. Somehow gym clothes, and gym activities, made a person feel even fatter than he was.

Phooey, he said to himself, deciding that Jeb and Otto looked pretty silly, bouncing around that way, holding their fists at fancy angles, trying to look as if they knew what they were doing. He glanced up at a "Martin?" and found Mr. Foran beside him.

"Yeah?" he said. "I mean, yeah, Mr. Foran?"

Mr. Foran smiled a little. "Want to box a bit with me?" he asked. "I used to be pretty good in college, believe it or not. I'll show you a few tricks about—"

"I think boxing's dumb," Martin interrupted. It

was funny how he'd hear himself saying things like that, and be sorry, and not even want to say them, but go ahead and say them anyway. Growing a little angry—maybe with himself and maybe not—he waved a hand toward the pugilists. "They look sappy."

"Oh, I don't know," Mr. Foran said. "They aren't too bad, considering their age."

Martin shrugged. Hearing other people praised wasn't his favorite way to spend recess.

Mr. Foran tilted his head up, blinked against the snowflakes. "Can't blame you for yelling out that way. The first fall of snow is always like a miracle, isn't it?" When Martin didn't reply, he went on, "Probably be sledding weather after school, wouldn't you say?"

"How should I know?"

For a second he thought Mr. Foran was going to walk away. And the fact was he couldn't blame him. What mean thing, Martin wondered, was in him that forced him to talk this way, be this way? Sometimes he felt really friendly, anxious to talk with people, maybe even, as now, learn a few tricks about boxing. But when the words came out—and since Rufus had gone he'd been worse—they sounded like this. It had gotten so they practically didn't talk to him at home at all. He'd find his mother or his father looking at him in that puzzled, unhappy way, and he'd wait for them to say or do something that would help him out, but whatever they tried to do or say, he'd just get angry, and it would end up in a fight, with Martin sent to his room and Marietta crowing.

Not all the time, not every time. But a lot. An awful lot.

"Yeah, I think maybe it'll be good for sledding," he said hurriedly to his teacher. "Looks like it will."

"Looks as if," said Mr. Foran.

And there you are, said Martin to himself. Nag, nag, nag—they can't do anything else.

"Does it annoy you to have your grammar corrected?" Mr. Foran asked. "I am a teacher, you know, Martin. Part of my job."

A bit taken aback at having his mind read so readily, Martin said, "It's okay. I mean, go ahead." For all the good it'll do you, he added to himself and then, looking at Mr. Foran, suspected that had been mind-read, too.

"Martin, let's skip the remaining twenty-one pages, shall we?"

Martin gaped.

"It wasn't a very judicious piece of discipline to

start with," Mr. Foran continued. "It was just— You know you can get a person pretty riled up, Martin."

Don't I know it, Martin thought. He said nothing.

"You've done an admirable job, so far," Mr. Foran said, and in spite of himself Martin felt a glow of pleasure. Hearing himself praised, during recess or any other time, was highly agreeable to him. "Admirable," Mr. Foran said again. "I'm sure your parents think so too."

"Parents?" said Martin.

"Surely they know how hard you've been working?"

"Why should they? I mean, I do my homework, that's all. What do they know about it?"

"You didn't tell them about this?" Mr. Foran asked, looking surprised.

Martin shook his head.

"You astound me. Why didn't you tell them?"

Martin thought for a moment. "I guess I figured it was my problem," he said at last.

The teacher studied him thoughtfully. "That's a very grown-up attitude," he said at length, and again Martin felt the warmth and pleasure that words of praise brought him. On the rare occasions when he got any, Martin always made up his mind to conduct himself in such a manner that people would be praising him all the time.

He could hear the voices saying, That Martin Hastings, really a remarkable boy, so intelligent, so popular, so interesting. For a while, you know, people misunderstood him. They didn't see what a fine young man he is. But now, of course, everyone knows. His parents are so proud. And that teacher, Mr. Foran, can't say enough good things about–

Smiling a little, filled with an almost unearthly sense of his own goodness and value, Martin stared through the falling snow. "Thanks," he said. Then, looking at Mr. Foran, added, "About the twenty-one copies, I mean. Boy, I'll be glad to be rid of those."

The bell rang, and Mr. Foran, with a parting pat on Martin's shoulder, went to collect his charges. Martin, following slowly, thought how you sure couldn't figure a grown-up. Cross as two sticks one day, sweet as honey the next. What was a person supposed to make of them?

But, warmed by the teacher's approval, Martin felt ready just now to forgive him all his faults. Maybe, he thought, in a flash of insight, they can't help being mixed up any more than kids can. This was a depressing thought, and it boded ill for the future, but Martin failed to be depressed. Because in that distant, just about unbelievable time when he himself became a grown-up, he would be different from the ones he knew. He wasn't going to be hurried and tired and quick-tempered, like his own father, or up one day and down the next, like Mr. Foran. He was going to be different, sensible.

"Wow, Marty," said Otto Sonberg, as they started up the stairs, "you sure did us a good turn today, yelping out like that."

"What do you mean, yelping?" Martin started to say, then checked himself. So he'd yelped. It had gotten them all an extra five minutes of freedom, hadn't it? The snow was traveling down more and more heavily.

"Want to come home with me after school?" he said suddenly to Otto. "I got two sleds."

Otto hesitated. They were both thinking about that visit to his house last fall, but neither referred to it. "Okay," he said finally. "Jeb's busy anyway. Music lesson. Sure, I'll come for a while."

Martin smiled happily and could hardly concentrate the rest of the afternoon. He was so impatient for the dismissal bell to ring that he couldn't sit still. He wriggled in his chair, slapped at imaginary insects, screwed up his face, yawned, stretched, almost fell asleep, and was brought to attention by Mr. Foran's exasperated voice.

"Martin, this is a classroom, not a dormitory. I'll thank you to wait until you are home to do your sleeping."

The boys snorted, the girls giggled, and Martin looked at his betrayer with disappointment.

When at last the dismissal bell rang, he jumped up and beat it to the locker room before Mr. Foran could make any alternative suggestion. He was not going to be kept in this afternoon, and that was that. Even if Mr. Foran *told* him to stay, he wouldn't. But Mr. Foran did not. He seemed to recognize that no authority is higher than that of the season's first snowfall, and he let them all go without a word.

Otto and Martin ran shouting up the hill. The snow, which had lessened during the early afternoon, had begun to fall heavily again. It lay along branches and porch steps and telephone wires, piling fuzzily, softly, on itself, covering lawns and sidewalks. In the streets, cars went by carefully, leaving black tire trails crossing and curving behind them.

Children scooped snow from the branches of firs and pines, fashioning snowballs that wouldn't quite hold together yet, but gave them more heady delight than any later ones would bring. Once, near home, Martin and Otto stood absolutely quiet and listened to the sound of the snow sweeping down. It was as if all those billions of snowflakes had billions of very tiny voices.

They went on, and dragged Martin's and Marietta's sleds out of the garage. Martin was pretty sure Marietta wouldn't come for hers. She'd gotten sort of dainty lately for anything as wild and cold as snow. But, even if she did, she was going to have a fat chance of getting it. He and Otto took the sleds and ran four blocks to a hill the police always shut off for sledders.

There were piles of people there already, and for the next couple of hours Martin was completely happy. He and Otto raced each other, sometimes went down together, trudged up again side by side, laughing and talking.

"Mr. Foran canceled the rest of those crummy papers for me," Martin said once, as they panted upward.

"He did, huh?" Otto nodded approvingly. "He's a good guy, Mr. Foran."

"Some*times*," Martin said with feeling.

"Nobody's a good guy all the time," Otto pointed out. At the top of the hill he turned and stared down. "Boy, I bet Jeb is boiling. Having to practice the piano with all this—" He spread his arms.

Martin didn't want to talk about Jeb. He was pretending that he and Otto were best friends, and the introduction of Jeb ruined the feeling.

"I wonder how old Rufus is," he said, to change the subject. Otto was intensely interested in Rufus, as he wanted a dog himself and didn't have one. Everybody, Martin thought, anyway every boy, wants a dog. Edward Frost was in a state of continual agitation, trying to get his parents to see how responsible he was (he wasn't, of course) so that they'd give in and get him a dog, any old dog. Edward had had some sharp words to say about how Martin had loused up everyone's chances by his failure to deserve and take care of Rufus. It seemed Mrs. Frost had pointed out that if a big boy like Martin couldn't be relied on how could Edward? This struck Martin as just another instance of grown-up sneakiness. Mrs. Frost would never in the world suggest that Martin could be reliable except to use it for her own advantage in depriving Edward of something. Still, that was

Edward's problem. Martin didn't think he'd deserve a dog if he lived to be ninety.

"I'll bet you," Otto said, "that Rufus is tearing around that farm right this minute like a crazy man. I mean, being so young, he's never seen snow before, has he?"

Martin, who thought he'd gotten over the worst of missing Rufus, had a sudden terrible pain, like a cramp. Snow, sledding, even Otto, all at once were unimportant. His dog was somewhere, running in the snow, wondering what it was, barking and wild the way dogs get in the snow, and Martin wasn't with him, couldn't see it, couldn't share it.

He could hear himself saying, It's snow, Rufe. All this cold white stuff is snow, and you can tear around in it all you like. He could almost *see* Rufus, standing before him, head turned slightly to listen, a little heap of snow on the black nose where he'd pushed it along the ground.

"What's the matter, Marty?" Otto said. "You gone into a trance? Let's go down again."

Martin shook himself, tried to smile. "Oh, okay. Sure. Let's go."

When they were too cold to descend the hill even once more, they walked home stiffly, blowing on frozen fingers, trying to brush their clothes off.

"I guess maybe we should have changed," Martin said uneasily.

"Yeah. I guess we maybe should have. My feet are freezing." Otto looked down, shook his head, and said, "Oh, murder. My good shoes. I forgot."

"We'll put them in the oven."

After they'd put their shoes in the oven and turned it to its highest point, they fixed some cocoa and, sitting on the living room floor, ate the cookies Mrs. Hastings had made for dinner.

"Look out for crumbs," Martin said virtuously. "Try to eat over the napkin."

"That's what I'm doing," Otto said. "Sure your mother won't mind us eating all these?"

"Heck no," said Martin expansively. He added a phrase his father used with guests, "Everything here is yours."

"Gee, thanks. These're good."

"Yeah. My mother's a good cook." It was nice to be able to show Otto that he didn't have the only mother who baked things for people.

"Where is she? Your mother, I mean?" Otto asked.

"Out. She's always out in the afternoon. She has a job."

"Oh. Do you like that?"

"Sort of. Leaves you free to do what you want. I hate people interfering with me all the time."

"So do I," Otto said eagerly. "What I mostly hate is how they never think they've said anything until they've said it six times."

"You can say that again," Martin replied appreciatively. "My mother doesn't ask me *once* in the morning if I've got my lunch money and if I remember my music lesson is today and all that. She asks sixty times, maybe more."

"And my father, if he tells me on Monday about a job I gotta do on Saturday, he spends the rest of the week *reminding* me that I gotta do it. You'd think we were deaf, or something."

Martin crowed. This was great, sharing the same feelings with someone.

"Only, they're okay, of course," Otto said, turning suddenly cautious. "Most of the time."

"Oh, sure," Martin said, without enthusiasm. "Sure thing."

Otto looked around the room. "What does your father do?" he asked.

"Sells insurance. What does yours?"

"He's a curator at the zoo."

"He *is?*" Martin said, enormously impressed. "Boy, that is something." You'd think he would have known this sooner, but that was what came of being around Mrs. Sonberg. You didn't find out anything except how nervous you made her. "You can get to go any time you want, huh?"

"Anybody can go to the zoo," Otto said. "It's free."

"No, but I mean you can go into the cages and all, can't you?"

"Sometimes," Otto said. "Some cages. I got to sit with the baby walrus a couple of times. He put his head right on my knees."

"He did?" said Martin, almost ill with envy.

"Yeah. But I wouldn't want to go in with the lions, like. Or the bear pits."

"Golly," Martin breathed, thinking what it would be like to have a baby walrus put its head on your knees. What a break, to have your father be a bigwig at the zoo. "I like animals better than people," he said suddenly.

"Do you?" Otto said, wrinkling his nose. "I like dogs. I mean, I'm crazy about them. And that walrus is a honey. But you can't like—say, a hyena, or like that."

"Even a hyena," Martin insisted excitedly. "And tigers and snakes and elephants and porcupines—"

"I guess you like them all, all right," Otto admitted.

"Did I ever tell you about the time I went swimming with the seals?" Martin asked abruptly.

"No, you didn't. And I don't believe you."

"No kidding, Otto. And right down there in your father's zoo." It never took Martin more than a second to get caught up in some fancy like this, and he could improvise endlessly.

"Tell me about it, then," Otto said, obviously not prepared to credit a single word.

"No, honest," Martin said. "I really did. See, I sneaked out of the house one night and bicycled down to the zoo—"

"You went ten miles on your bike at night?" Otto burst out.

"Nothing to that," Martin said modestly. "I've biked more than fifty." He, at least, was believing every word. "So when I got there, it was all dark, and nobody around but me and the animals—"

"They have guards patrolling there at night. All the time."

"Then they must've just finished their inspection of the seal pool," Martin said quickly. "Anyway,

I climbed over the fence and slid into the pool—"

"In your clothes?" Otto said, suspicious but willing, in a way, to be convinced.

"I wore bathing trunks under my pants. So I took off my pants and shoes and shirt, and slid into the pool, and just swam around for ages.

Otto grinned. "How did the seals like it?"

"Oh, they liked it fine. Seals are very fond of humans, you know. We tossed that big red ball back and forth, and a few times there," he added in a rush of inspiration, "I just wrapped my arms around one of those seals and sailed right down to the bottom of the pool and then up and down again, over and over. Oh, it was great, just great—"

He could feel the warm velvety body of the seal against his own body, feel the rush of water as he and the seal curved through swaying black waters, down and down, and then in a flying arc up again to burst through the surface of the water. What was having a baby walrus put its head on your knees compared to this?

"Boy, you really take the cake," Otto said, his face a mixture of astonishment, distrust, and faint belief. As if he wanted to believe it, because it sounded so good. Suddenly he lifted his head, sniffed, and said, "Marty! Our shoes!"

They dashed into the kitchen. Black, smelly smoke was seeping around the edges of the oven door. Martin threw it open and gasped.

"Oh, crimers. *Look.*"

They snatched their scorched, steaming, curling shoes from the cavern and threw them to the floor, where they lay sending up tendrils of smoke. The toes, practically to the laces, turned back in a Turkish manner. Soles and heels were blackened and smelled horrible. Their eyes smarting from the smell and the smoke, the two boys studied this disaster.

"That was a great idea," Otto said at last. "Just great."

"Well, you agreed," Martin said, defending himself weakly. They were his good shoes, too. Or had been. He leaned down, picked up one of Otto's, and tried to force the front part flat. The melting rubber of the heel stuck to his fingers, and the odor in the kitchen was getting worse by the second.

"You better turn that oven off," Otto said, and did it himself. "Some of the rubber must be stuck in there," he decided, holding his nose.

"I don't think you're going to be able to walk in these," Martin said morosely. "Not till the heels harden, or something. You'll stick to the ground."

"I won't be able to walk in them then, unless I break my feet in the middle. I mean, my feet just don't turn up that way."

"Maybe if we ran them under the water we could flatten them out."

Otto sighed heavily. "We could try, I suppose."

Deciding that cold water might crack the leather, they filled the sink with lukewarm water and plunged the two pairs of shoes in, trying to manipulate them back to normal. It seemed to help slightly.

"Marty, I never saw anybody like you," Otto said without rancor. "Everything you do turns out wrong."

Martin, full of dull foreboding, said drearily, "I know."

Who was going to be maddest? His own parents, or Otto's? He could have talked his way out of the cookies, probably. He'd already made up his mind how. He would have said that he was treating a guest the way his father did, and after all they couldn't jump on him for that. Or maybe they couldn't. But the cookies weren't going to count for much after his mother got a look at these shoes.

"Hey, I just thought of something," Otto said.

"What?" Martin asked nervously.

"How am I supposed to get home? I mean, it's late, and I oughta go. But what do I put on my feet?" He picked a shoe out of the sink and let the water gush from it. Now it was not only bent, but soaking.

Oh, golly, Martin thought. He felt baffled and overwhelmed. Why hadn't they left the shoes alone when there was only snow on them? They could have put them *near* the oven or on top. They could have–

"Marty, will you answer me?"

"I'm trying to think."

"My mother's going to be hopping."

Martin, too well aware of that, said nothing.

"She probably won't let me come here any more," Otto went on.

"Do you have to tell where you were?" Martin asked without much hope.

"Do you want me to lie?"

That was just what Martin wanted, but he saw that there was no point in asking. It wouldn't do any good, anyway, since Otto apparently didn't have much experience in lying. As an expert in the subject, Martin could tell that.

"Won't she know it wasn't our fault?" he asked anxiously. "I mean, we were just trying to get the darn things dry."

"All I know is they're my good shoes. And all I know furthermore is they're soaking wet. I wear these home, and I not only catch heck, I catch pneumonia."

"Hey," Martin said suddenly, "how about if you borrow my dad's boots? Come on." He ran to the hall closet, rummaged around on the floor, came up with his father's galoshes. "Be sort of big on you, but better than nothing, I guess."

"I can stuff newspapers in the toes, maybe."

"Sure, Otto. That's just the thing. That'll keep them on. Then you can carry the shoes, and put them in the closet when your mother isn't looking. Maybe by morning they'll be all right."

"Something tells me these shoes aren't ever going to be all right," Otto said glumly.

"Listen," Martin said, assailed by another wave of apprehension. "Listen, Otto, be *sure* you bring those galoshes back tomorrow. And I do mean bring them *back*."

"Keep your shirt on."

"I don't care about my shirt, just so I keep track of Dad's boots," Martin said, attempting a laugh.

But Otto, feeling more and more desperate about the immediate future, didn't even smile. "I better go," he said, and left without even a good-bye.

Martin went into the kitchen, breathed tentatively, found the stench almost as bad as at first. He threw open the windows, letting in a rush of cold air that carried a burden of snowflakes with it. Emptying the sink and then washing it carefully, Martin wrapped his shoes in some newspaper, took them upstairs to his room and shoved them to the back of the closet. He got into his old shoes and hoped his mother wouldn't notice.

When she came in, all she noticed was the swirl of air currents coming from the kitchen and spreading through the house.

"What's going on here?" she called out. "Martin? Marietta? Where are you?"

"Here I am, Mom," said Martin, sidling out of his room and down the stairs. "You want me for something? I can run an errand, or something?"

"Did you open these kitchen windows?"

Martin snapped his fingers. "Gee whiz, I forgot to close them, didn't I?"

His mother went to the kitchen and threw the windows down. "Will you please tell me what the reason was? Why would you open the windows in the middle of winter and go off and leave them?" she asked her son, who'd followed her in, sniffing from side to side like a bloodhound.

"It seemed a bit stuffy in here," Martin explained. There were sort of sooty marks all around the edges of the oven door, but the smell was pretty much gone. "I had a friend home after school," he said, sounding proud. "I know you don't like me to," he added hastily, "but Otto's not a sloppy guy—"

"Martin," she interrupted, "don't explain that way. I'm *glad* you had a friend here. Really glad. I think it's wonderful for you."

She sounded too glad. As if she'd forgotten everything she'd warned him about concerning boys alone in a house. Everybody knows I don't really have friends, Martin thought. Pretending you don't care doesn't fool them. He looked at his mother, who was being pretty gentle, for her, and wondered why she couldn't always be this way. She didn't even get mad about the cookies, although she didn't look too happy when he explained that they'd eaten them all. "You know," he told her eagerly, "how Dad always tells guests that the house is theirs, so I thought—"

"But these were for dinner."

"But Mrs. Sonberg always gives guys cookies or cake or stuff. I mean, what was I supposed to do? There they were on the table. Could I tell Otto he couldn't have any, we want to eat them all ourselves? Holy cow."

"That's enough, Martin. Next time you might leave a few for dinner."

Next time, Martin thought miserably. What next time? But he said that he would, and that was that. He could not bring himself to mention the shoes.

It snowed all night. The next morning it looked like the Antarctic. Martin, waking to this wonder, lay in bed enjoying the look of soft white triangles that drifted up his window panes. Beyond, on the tree branches, the snow was piled up, glittering in the sun.

Through his closed door he heard his father shout, "Marion, where are my galoshes?"

"In the downstairs closet, aren't they?" Mrs. Hastings answered.

Martin, feeling suddenly icy, as if he'd been left outdoors all night, pulled the covers over his head and lay there suffocating, trying to think. He ought, and he knew it, to get up and go downstairs and explain where the galoshes now were. His father was getting into a temper. His mother was upset because his father was. And every passing second increased the chance of his father's being late for work. Mr. Hastings did not like to be late for work.

Martin pushed the covers down, took a deep breath, sat up in bed, and opened his mouth to call out, just as the door flew open and his father appeared on the threshold.

"Martin! Do you know anything about my galoshes? Where are they?"

Whatever Martin had been going to say, he forgot it immediately. The bare thought of telling people now just where those galoshes had got to seemed to him plain crazy. He could just hear himself saying, They're at Otto's.

Otto? his father would yell. Otto who? What's Otto got to do with my boots? Speak up, Martin!

Martin, far from speaking up, only managed to shake his head. He started to pull the covers up again, because it was cold in the room.

"What are you doing?" his father said impatiently. "Get up. You're late. And, blast it, I'm going to be late, too." He turned and stamped down the stairs.

Martin, coughing nervously, crawled out of bed. They didn't suspect, that was plain. In all his borrowing, he had never had the nerve before to borrow something of his father's, so it hadn't occurred to them. Yet.

Having looked in all the probable places, like closets, they were now searching under chairs, behind doors, and even in the fireplace, where naturally they knew the galoshes wouldn't be.

Martin went into the bathroom to wash, since he didn't have to look to know where the galoshes were or were not.

"I tell you, Marion," his father was shouting, "I have to get going. How can I go out in this without galoshes? I'll get pneumonia. There must be three feet of snow out there."

"It's a good thing men don't wear open-toed shoes, isn't it, Daddy?" Marietta said in her cute voice. At the sound of it, Martin, washing his teeth, curled back his lips, exposing his teeth widely. He looked at himself in the mirror, finding this horrible face interesting.

Mr. Hastings, at this hour, under these circumstances, was not amused by Marietta. He growled something at her, then shouted up the stairs.

"Martin! Come here!"

Martin inched down the hallway to the head of the stairs.

His father, at the foot of the stairs, glared upward. "Look me in the eye," he said to his son, "and tell me you don't know where those boots have got to."

Balanced a moment between truth and falsehood, Martin made what seemed to him the only possible choice. He shook his head and said, "I don't know anything about them at all, Dad. Maybe you left them out on the back porch the last time it snowed, and a tramp took them, or something."

"The last time it snowed was about eight months ago," Mr. Hastings pointed out sharply.

"Well, rained then. The last heavy rain. Anyway, *I* don't know, Dad. Honest."

Mr. Hastings' eyes seemed to bore even more deeply into Martin's as he said, "Is that the truth you're telling me, Martin?"

*Crums,* Martin thought, wondering—as he always did at times like this—whether his father might possibly be able to see into his head, and taking the risk that he couldn't. *Crums.* What did they expect? That you'd lie and then *tell* them so?

He spread his hands in a gesture of innocence. "Honest," he said again. "I don't know where they are. Maybe you left them at the office."

Mr. Hastings, taking time for a final glare, dived

back into the closet and emerged with his rubber fishing boots. In spite of his uneasiness, Martin had to cover his mouth to keep from laughing. His father was going out in those? To the office?

"Daddy!" Marietta said shrilly. "You can't!"

"Oh, can't I?" Mr. Hastings sat down on the stairs, took off his shoes, and said to his wife as he pulled on the hip boots, "Put those in a bag for me, will you, Marion?"

Mrs. Hastings picked up the shoes and stood biting her lip. "Dear," she began, "are you quite sure—"

Mr. Hastings stood up looking wildly peculiar with his bowler hat, his dispatch case, and the hip boots disappearing under his town overcoat.

"Daddy, you look like a freak!" Marietta wailed.

"I presume," Mr. Hastings said icily, "that you'd all rather have me take my death of cold? *May* I have my shoes in a bag, please, Marion? Marietta, stop whining."

He trudged out, slamming the door behind him. In a moment they heard the garage doors sail up, and the sound of his car motor, sluggish and unwilling to turn over.

Marietta and Mrs. Hastings in the hallway, Martin at the top of the stairs, all held their breath as the churning engine spat, coughed, died, sparked suddenly to life, and Mr. Hastings backed through snow to the plowed street.

"I swear," said Mrs. Hastings half aloud, "if we had a long driveway, I'd put the house on the market this minute. Marietta, run in to breakfast. Martin, you'd better hurry. Goodness, what a morning. . . ."

Otto remembered to bring the galoshes to school, and that afternoon Martin stuffed them with snow, then brought them in and swore to his mother that he'd found them out back, buried under yesterday's snowfall.

"See," he said. "I was right. They were there all the time."

His mother looked at him narrowly, but by now Martin was so convinced of his own truthfulness that he felt honestly insulted.

"Boy," he muttered. "Some people don't get believed by anybody, not even their mother."

Mr. and Mrs. Hastings said no more about the boots. Unless they had actually been able to figure out what *had* happened, they were sort of stuck with Martin's story.

Whew, he said to himself that night in his room. Wow.

He decided he'd really better quit borrowing things. It occurred to him that he ought to stop lying, too. Or, anyway, ought to try. It seemed to Martin that a person could hardly get through life without lying some. But apparently Otto didn't need to. Or Jeb. He'd never heard Edward Frost described as a liar. Martin couldn't quite see how they managed it, but he made up his mind to try, really seriously try, to stop lying. Perhaps a person could get in the habit of telling the truth, just as he could get in the habit of not telling it. There'd be one thing, anyway, about always being truthful. You wouldn't have to try to remember what you'd said the last time.

Otto's mother, of course, was furious about the shoes. And, of course, she put the blame on Martin. But at least she didn't telephone his house, having gotten so little satisfaction out of that the last time. Otto, himself, was pretty distant with Martin for quite a long time. That hurt, in a way. Mostly because they'd had so much fun in the beginning of the afternoon.

As to his own shoes, Martin rubbed them vigorously with saddle soap and after a few days of discomfort worked them back practically to normal.

The rest of his life was normal, too, he supposed.

The normal number of fights, problems, nightmares. The normal amount of defending himself against the grown-ups and trying to find a place among the people his own age. Sometimes he seemed to be gaining, and sometimes he fell so far back it all seemed useless.

Old Huck Finn would have run away from so much trouble and frustration. Martin had to stay and worry his out somehow. And he couldn't help thinking how much easier it all would have been with Rufus. He thought that if he had still had Rufus he maybe wouldn't have had the other problems at all. He could have talked them out with his dog.

Without the dog, there really was no one to talk to. No one.

# PART TWO

# CHAPTER 5

"People, listen to me!" Martin said at dinner one night, getting his shout in before Marietta had a chance to launch out on one of her descriptions of what someone was wearing lately and why couldn't she have the same thing. "Listen, there's gonna be an assembly next week, the night before spring vacation starts. Everybody's doing skits and things, and I want you to come. You, too," he said kindly to Marietta, "if you want to."

"Why in the world would I—" Marietta began, and was interrupted by her mother.

"What night, Martin?"

"Friday. A week from Friday."

"Oh, but Mama—"

"Marietta, wait a second, please," Mrs. Hastings warned. She turned back to Martin. "I'm sorry, but Marietta asked me quite a while ago to chaperone that evening at a Fortnightly. I can't disappoint her now."

"But that isn't fair!" Martin burst out. "You're always not disappointing her. Why don't you not disappoint me for a change?"

"You didn't ask me in time."

"She's always getting things done for her. You went to her dopey old play, all right, I noticed. But when *I* ask—"

"Martin, stop yammering," Mr. Hastings said. "Can't you ever ask for something quietly and politely? It's like living next to a sidewalk drill, your voice."

"Quietly and politely never got you there either. Nothing makes anybody go to my nights at school."

"That isn't true, Martin."

"Well, when did you go then? Huh? When?"

Mr. Hastings looked uncomfortable. "I went to Parents' Open House last year," he said at last.

"The year before," Martin said, almost beside himself. "The year *before.*"

"Then last year I must have been unavoidably prevented."

"That's what I'm *saying.* You're always unavoidably prevented when it's something of mine. Why don't you get unavoidably prevented when it's Marietta's turn? You *both* went to her play."

"Marty, do you actually believe what you're saying? That we favor your sister over you?"

You bet your life I do, Martin thought. But he didn't answer directly. "How about last summer?" he said. "How about camp, when there was only enough money to send one of us? Who got to go, huh? Me or her?"

"We told you that next time you could go."

"Thanks a bunch," Martin mumbled. Next summer was too far off to consider, and anyway, it was that Marietta went *first,* all the time, that she always came first . . . that was what got him so mad. And they never would admit it, never would—

"That play was the first affair of Marietta's that we've been to all year," Mr. Hastings was saying. He seemed to realize, all at once, that this answer was not going to satisfy Martin and might launch Marietta on some complaints of her own, so he added quickly, "What you and your sister don't seem to understand is that your mother and I are tired at night."

Martin, and Marietta, remained unimpressed.

"Will you consider that I put in practically a

twelve-hour day, and your mother, by the time she's finished working at her job and here too, puts in more than that? When night comes, we're too exhausted to get out the car and drive down and spend two or three hours on those incredibly uncomfortable chairs. It isn't that we don't want to attend your festivities, don't you see?"

Martin thought that probably other parents—the Frosts, the Sonbergs, the Grahams—were tired at night, too. But it seemed pointless to argue, because his father wasn't too tired to go to assemblies. He was too bored. Martin had heard him say so.

"Skip it," he said. "I don't really care anyway." Expecting to be sent from the table for rudeness, he half pushed back his chair.

"Martin, wait." Mr. Hastings sighed and did look tired. "We're certainly not aware of doing more things for Marietta than for you. I hope you believe that."

He waited, but Martin said nothing.

"Well, it's the truth," Mr. Hastings went on. "I guess perhaps it's just that Marietta has a—nicer way of asking. The fact is, people can't help responding to courtesy. And parents are people, whether you believe it or not."

Martin had nothing to say to that either.

"Anyway, the whole thing's academic. Your mother has to do that chaperoning for Marietta, and I'm going to be out of town that night. If I weren't, believe me I'd be happy to go."

He's sure asking me to believe a lot of stuff, Martin said to himself. Well, I don't. I don't believe any of it.

"What are you going to do in the assembly, Martin?" Mrs. Hastings asked.

"What do you care?"

"Martin!" his father said warningly.

"Well, what does she?" Martin demanded, throwing caution to the winds. "Nobody cares what I do in this family!"

He jumped up, his chair crashing backward to the floor, and ran to his room, where he sat breathing hard, waiting for his father to bellow up the stairs.

After a while his breathing subsided, and no summons came of any sort. No one spoke to him again that night. Instead of finding this a relief, it only convinced Martin more completely that they just didn't care about him at all.

The next day he crashed a doll's tea party that Ruth Ann Silver was giving in her backyard. He drank all the ginger ale (that was the tea) and then went down the street and wrote nasty words on Mr. Eckman's sidewalk. On the way back he pushed Edward Frost's bicycle over and left it with wheels spinning wildly.

Mrs. Silver came surging up to the house that evening to tell Martin's parents how they ought to lock him in an attic until he came of age. Mr. Hastings practically threw her off the porch, after which he belted Martin, took some bicarbonate of soda, and went to his room to rest. Mrs. Hastings had to deal with Mr. Eckman when *he* came. The Frosts didn't appear.

And so it went for the rest of the week. Martin knocked down Edward or his bike or both just about every day, sent a lot of hats skimming into trees, got kept in four times for sassing Mr. Foran, was sent to the principal for tripping up a girl in the hall, and even managed to pick a real fight with Otto Sonberg.

Martin had been sitting in the yard during recess, reading some comics. He'd given up real books, because if he read books it pleased his mother and father. Comics drove them crazy, so he was filling his room with them, buying old copies off guys who'd finished with them. The fact was, he found them sort of dopey, but as long as it bugged his parents he was willing to stick with them.

Otto had come by and asked if he wanted to play volleyball after school. It was the first time Otto had asked him to do anything in ages, and for a moment Martin responded gladly. But then he decided he'd had enough of Otto's kindness. Who did the guy think he was, anyway, the director of a boys' club?

"I'm busy after school. That's when I'm going to run away," he told Otto, and tried not to look surprised at his own words.

"Run away?" said Otto, sounding interested. "Run away where?"

"To sea," said Martin, because he couldn't think of anything else. And yet, as he spoke, he realized it was just what he was going to do. Ship out as a cabin boy and never come back. He could see himself, standing at attention before the captain, his face composed and alert, his uniform immaculate. "You're a good man, Hastings," the captain would be saying. "I wouldn't be at all surprised if you made first mate pretty soon." "Aye, aye, sir," Martin would say crisply and turn on his heel to hurry back to his bunk, where he'd be studying Morse code and celestial navigation in his spare time.

"You can't run away to sea without a union card," Otto snorted, picking up one of the comics.

"Boy, you think you know everything, don't you?" Martin said angrily. "It just so happens that I have a—an uncle who's a ship's captain out of Gloucester."

"In a pig's eye you have."

"How do you know what kind of uncle I have?" Martin demanded.

"I just do know, that's all. If you had an uncle who was a sea captain, we'd have heard about it by now, Marty old boy. You've got an uncle who's a sea captain like you went swimming with the seals that time. Everything's in your fat head."

"You gimme that," Martin said, snatching and tearing the comic book. "And leave my things alone, see?"

"Boy, I can leave you and your things alone easy as falling off a log," Otto said, getting up. He walked away, toward Jeb McCrae, who'd been waiting for him. The two of them looked over at Martin and laughed.

WORLD
Super Boy

"I told you," Jeb said loudly. "What d'ya want to waste your time on him for, anyway?"

"I just thought the poor dope might like to play with us, is all," said Otto, shrugging. "Let's go, Jeb."

Martin scrabbled his comic books together with shaking fingers and went up to the empty classroom, where he sat at his desk wondering what to do next. He wouldn't run away, because he'd be afraid to. The honesty of which he was often capable made him admit that. Tom Sawyer, Huck, they'd do it in a minute. But Martin Hastings? No. He put his head in his hands and wondered if he'd ever get away from them all—his family, his teachers, his so-called friends. He wished he could shove ten years behind him in a minute. In ten years he'd be gone so far they wouldn't find him with radar and a platoon of detectives.

If they looked.

"Martin? Don't you feel well?"

It was Mr. Foran, come up to the room early too.

Martin lifted his head, considered an assortment of lies, then said simply, "Not so awfully, Mr. Foran."

"What's the trouble?"

The trouble? Crums . . . He'd have to write another paper to cover that. "Everything, I guess."

"Could I help?"

"I don't think so."

"Sometimes talking is a help."

"I talk too much as it is," Martin said glumly.

"I'm looking forward to hearing your bugle solo in assembly tomorrow night," the teacher said. Martin shrugged. "Are you practicing?"

"I don't know. I guess so." He felt funny, about fifty times his weight and as if, somehow, he was nailed to the chair.

"You're a good bugler, Martin. Do you ever go to camp?"

"My sister goes."

After a silence Mr. Foran said, "I guess your parents will be proud when they hear you."

"They'll have to have awfully good ears. My mother's chaperoning for my sister, and my father's going to be in Cedar Rapids."

"Oh. I see. Well, I'm going to be proud of you, if that helps."

Martin knew he should say it would, but somehow the words wouldn't come. Just about every other kid in the school would have a parent, some even two parents and grandparents, there. They'd be proud even if their kid fell flat on his face. That was how parents were. Except his. He wanted to thank Mr. Foran, but he couldn't.

The bell rang, pupils returned to their desks, classes resumed, ended, and Martin as usual walked home alone. Even when he had a chance to rush Edward Frost in Edward's own backyard, just when the dumbbell was climbing out of a tree where he'd hung a birdhouse, it didn't make Martin feel much better.

Mrs. Frost saw them out of her window and called Edward in. And she didn't call Mrs. Hastings about it either. Probably, Martin figured, the Frosts had gotten tired of complaining. Probably, Martin said to himself, they were just tired of him, period. For some crazy reason, this bothered him more than when they were always fuming around, grumbling and threatening.

On the way to school the next day—Friday, assembly day—Martin spied Edward ahead of him, carrying a box carefully under his arm. Martin began to run, and Edward, hearing without even looking around, took to his heels, toward Rod Graham's house. It was no trick catching up with him, blocking his way.

"*Good* morning, Weird One," said Martin. "What have you got in the box, huh?"

"Dynamite," Edward said nervously. "You touch it, and we'll both be blown up, Fatso."

Martin, who'd been going to say something airy and let Edward go, was abruptly swamped with rage. "Oh, yeah?" he said nastily. "You're a real funny little man, aren't you?"

Edward hugged the box closer to his chest and said nothing.

"*Aren't you?*" Martin growled.

He could feel his blood racing, throbbing in his head. He was so darned sick of being jabbed at and needled, so tired of being made fun of, that he could hardly think. In one way he recognized that Edward, so much smaller, was no worthy target. He also, in a boy's way, admired Edward's spunkiness. But these considerations vanished in the fog of his anger. Small and spunky though he was, Edward represented at this moment all of Martin's enemies and tormentors.

"Well now," he drawled, and he could feel each word slide separately from his lips. "I just guess you'd better say uncle. Just for practice, like."

As he spoke he grabbed the box and dashed

it to the ground. From it spilled a bright red costume. Edward's get-up for the assembly, of course. And, of course, it would be something Mrs. Frost had made for him, the way she made cookies, and time, and everything else for her son. Martin, slowly and deliberately, put his foot on the scarlet overall and waited.

"Uncle," Edward said at last.

Martin stepped back, smiled, and swaggered off whistling. That would show Edward Frost, *and* his mother, and everyone in the school, and—everyone in the world. That would show them.

There was no school that afternoon. In their separate classrooms each class went through a dress rehearsal of its particular skit to be presented to parents and guests in the evening.

Parents and guests, Martin thought, laughing to himself. He'd bet it was all anyone could do to drag one parent, much less somebody else, to the school on these evenings. He said as much to Otto, who looked surprised and said, "My next-door neighbor is coming. Mr. Phillips. He wants to see me be the tough sergeant."

Martin had nothing to say. It just passed belief, and it certainy defied comment. It was probably why Otto was so pleasant to people all the time.

People were always pleasant to him. Watching Otto get into his sergeant's costume, Martin wondered what it would be like to have everybody nice to you. To have everybody like you.

The sixth-grade boys were presenting a comic skit. A morning at a boot training camp. Martin, as the only bugler, was to blow reveille. Otto was the sergeant who yelled everybody around, and Jeb and the others were recruits who wouldn't get up, made mistakes, mixed up the sergeant, and were, generally, pretty funny. The girls, who were doing some ballet thing as their skit, watched while the boys rehearsed, and it certainly made *them* laugh. In fact, it had the boys themselves laughing so hard they could scarcely act.

Reveille, which Martin had been practicing for weeks, came out smooth as syrup. All the guys, for a moment, looked at Martin with respect when the last note died away.

"Man, that is *good,*" said Jeb McCrae. "You ought to join a band, or something."

"With a bugle?" Martin said, laughing a little, but flushed with pleasure and pride.

"Whyn't you get a sax, or something, Marty?" Otto said. "I bet you'd be a sensation."

"Maybe I will," Martin said excitedly.

He could see himself—dressed in a red dinner jacket, standing up there before swooning crowds, making that old saxophone swing like it had never swung before. People would crowd around him afterward, trying to get a word in, trying to shake his hand. Everybody would be there. He could hear himself laughing, shaking the hands, looking at his parents, who would come to *this* affair, all right. And maybe then they'd remember how he had begged and pleaded for someone to—

"Martin, that was very impressive," said Mr. Foran. "But if you will now come out of your dream and get with the rest of us, perhaps we can finish up in time for you all to go home early. Remember now, class," he said, turning from Martin to the room in general, "you are to be here half an hour before the guests arrive. As all the classes will be giving their skits before us—" Some faces drooped, and Mr. Foran, with a smile, said, "It is only right that, as the oldest, you should give the grand finale." They brightened at that, seeing how right he was. "And, naturally," Mr. Foran continued, "as the oldest, you can be relied upon to behave the best throughout the evening."

Did he, or did he not, look again at Martin as he spoke? Martin couldn't be sure. He was still too enraptured by the vision of himself, that red dinner jacket, and the saxophone he'd now decided he absolutely had to have. He would work around the house as he'd never worked before in order to get one. He'd go out and find a job this summer. He'd give up camp, if they offered to send him. He'd promise them anything and even try to keep the promises. He saw now, and could not understand why he had never realized it before, that what he needed to make everything all right was a saxophone.

Caught up in this dream of the future, the present became somehow less important. Even the fact that tonight he would be performing alone—well, anyway, not with his parents there—didn't matter so much. He felt so set up and confident that on the way home he ignored Rod Graham, who popped out from behind a tree and yelled, "Ya big balloon. Why don't you go somewhere and bust?"

Martin clutched his bugle case tighter and kept walking. At home he took the stairs two at a time. He was going to take a good long shower before dinner and get out his clean clothes, all ready to put on afterward.

There was a sign on Marietta's door. Martin walked over, curious to see what it was this time.

Marietta was given to posting her room like a hunting preserve. As if anyone wanted to go in it.

DANGER! KEEP OUT! THIS MEANS YOU, DOPUS.

Since he never went in her room and had no intention of doing so now, Martin shrugged. Who *wanted* to go in a place that reeked of ribbons and perfume from Woolworth's? She wasn't even fourteen and she'd never had a real date in her life, only dancing school or birthday party ones, but she and those dumb friends of hers spent all their time dressing up, fiddling with their hair, talking about boys as if they really knew some.

Martin studied the sign and had to laugh. She went around all the time trying to act eighteen, at least, and then stuck something like this on her door. Eight was more like it.

Suddenly, and only because he was in such high spirits, he decided to play a little joke on her. He went into his room, got a red crayon, reversed Marietta's sign, and wrote, "HELP, HELP, TO MY RESUCUE ANYBODY!"

He read it, as if in discovery—being a person who always acted thoroughly—then threw her door open and rushed in shouting, "Take heart! I am here! Where's the foul fiend who's frightening you? Just let him show his face!"

Marietta turned furiously from her dressing table, where she had the lights on brightly and all her meager store of cosmetics spread around. "What are you doing, Marty? Get out!"

"But—" Martin began. "But—" He couldn't go on. Doubling up laughing, beating his hands together, he pointed at her helplessly. "Oh, golly, oh, crimers . . . oh, what a sight, what a sight—"

"Martin, you miserable little pill, get out of here!"

Collecting himself somewhat, Martin pointed to the open door and the sign.

"Sister dear, it appeals for help. I was just coming to your aid, like."

"I didn't write that, and you know it!"

"Oh, now, Sis. It's on your door, nessy pa? Nessy pa is French for—"

"Don't call me Sis! And get out. And you know darn well that if I wanted to write rescue, I'd know how to spell it."

"Listen, Sis, there's something wrong with your face, did you know? It's got smeared somehow. Did you tumble into the catsup?" He began to shake with laughter. She really was so funny looking it'd make a horse laugh. Didn't she know?

Martin clapped his hand to his brow, as if in

sudden enlightenment. "Oh!" he cried out. "Don't tell me I've made another gaffe. That's a French word, too. It means gaffe. And I have! A perfectly ghoulish gaffe. That's *make-up* on your face, isn't it? Not catsup at all. You are practicing the art of feminine wiles—"

Marietta, cheeks flaming with rouge and fury, picked up her hairbrush and started for him. No longer laughing, just for a moment Martin thought he'd let her come and then let her have it. But common sense reached him in time, and the realization of what his father would do if—no, when—Marietta told on him. He was in enough trouble around this house already without adding assault.

"Boy, you sure can't take a joke, can you?" he said in a weak attempt to minimize things.

"I can't take anything about you, jokes or anything else, see?" said Marietta, still brandishing the hairbrush.

"That goes—" Double was not nearly enough. "That goes ninetuple for me, let me tell you."

"There's no such thing as ninetuple, you silly dope."

"That's all *you* know. Boy, the day I see the last of you, I'm going to send up a rocket."

"Well, I hope you go with it and get into orbit and *never* land."

Their insults followed a sort of pattern, neither wanting to be the first to give in, but both tiring somewhat, growing bored with the necessity of being last. Even in their own ears there didn't seem to be much spirit or originality in their thrusts. Sometimes Martin thought of splendidly cutting things to say, after he'd got back to his room, but then the next time he and Marietta had a row he either couldn't work them in or forgot what they'd been.

Today, after he'd closed his door, a whole sentence popped into his mind.

Marietta, he said, not quite aloud, you look like a moldy mackerel, and if you think a face like that is going to get you a boyfriend, then you're so far in left field you're out of the ball park. It's more likely to get you first prize at a Halloween party, or in jail.

This struck him as richly comical, and he almost went across the hall to yell it at her door. On second thought, it seemed like too much trouble, and besides, his mother came in at that moment.

"Mama!" Marietta yelled, running down the stairs. "Mama! I want to tell you something."

*Oh, murder,* Martin said to himself. He went out on the landing to catch the scene.

"What is it?" Mrs. Hastings asked her daughter. "Hurry up, dear. I have to get dinner started, and I'm late. If I'm to get dinner done and get ready for your party in time . . ." She didn't finish the sentence, only sighed and yawned and said, "You know, I've practically forgotten what my family looks like. This job—"

"Mama, Martin's been bullying me again."

"It seems to me there's more and more work each day, and I get home later and later, and that's a fact."

"Mama, don't you care anything about me at all?"

"Oh, for heaven's sake, Marietta. Must you rush at me with complaints the minute I step in the door?"

"I only meant can't you listen to me instead of talking about your job all the time?"

Martin opened his mouth to protest that, closed it again for fear of being involved.

"I mean," Marietta was going on, "you said yourself you practically don't recognize your family, and you aren't ever home if someone needs you—"

"Marietta, stop nagging. I'm tired and in no

mood for it. Did you remember to get the potatoes scrubbed and in the oven? It's your night to set the table. Did you do it?" Silence from Marietta. "I take it that means no. All right, Marietta, do get out of my way so I can get started."

"But, Mama—"

"And please wash your face before your father gets in. You know how he hates to see little girls trying to act older than their age."

"I am not a little girl," Marietta said furiously.

"You are in our eyes," said Mrs. Hastings in a voice that forbade discussion.

It also, Martin thought, finishes that complaint for the moment. With all his mother had to do, she wouldn't get a second to listen before midnight. He felt sorry for his mother, working all day and coming in to arguments, dinner, and then having to go to that dumb Fortnightly and sit on a chair against the wall trying to look pleased.

As Marietta stamped upstairs he said, "By the way, just for your future reference—when you start to tell Dad about me busting into your room, I'm gonna tell him about that gook you smear all over your face in school. Don't worry, I've seen you, and up till now I haven't said anything. But don't think

I won't. And I'll tell him about the way you call guys on the telephone."

"Why, you worm. You miserable flea, you. What are you doing listening to my private conversations?"

"Private?" Martin snorted. "A person could hear that baby-talk squeal of yours in a Polaris sub under the North Pole." He lifted his own voice imitatively. "Oh, *Peter,* do tell me what the *Eng*lish homework is, I lost my *note*book, and *Peter, do* you like me best, I'll just die if you don't. . . ."

Martin dropped into his own tones, enjoying the look of despair on his sister's face. "I happen to know that Peter Brown is crazy about Pat Carson. He hangs around her house like a tick, is what I heard—"

Marietta went into her room, slamming the door so hard that Mrs. Hastings came out of the kitchen and called up the stairs, "What's going on up there? What was that?"

"I don't know," said Martin. "Just Marietta, retiring to her room."

"What's she trying to do, bring the house down?"

"Maybe so. I guess you got her mad."

Marietta flew into the hall. "Mama! That's not so! It was Marty. He—He—I wasn't slamming the door at you, I was only—"

"Oh, argue it out between you," said Mrs. Hastings wearily. "Goodness, how I wish there could be just a little peace and quiet around here. Just a little friendliness between you two—" She walked away, her fingers at her temples.

Martin felt again that rush of pity. He guessed it was pretty hard to work the way his mother did and come home to this. He stood biting his lip, and then, on an impulse he could not have explained, said to his sister, "I'm sorry, Marietta."

To his intense surprise Marietta, instead of lashing out at him again, began to cry. She just stood there, tears running down her face, not speaking.

"Oh, heck, now," Martin said uncomfortably. "I wasn't that bad. I mean, it isn't anything that hasn't happened before. Cut it out, Marietta. They'll say I've been beating you up again."

"Oh, it isn't you. It's . . . it's everything. They never let me do anything. You get away with murder, and I'm sat on no matter what I do."

At this absolutely astonishing version of their respective situations, Martin could only gape.

"Well, it's true," Marietta insisted, sniffling. "What if I do want to wear a little lipstick, or even call a boy on the phone? What's wrong with that? All the girls do it. I'm fourteen, and they treat me like a *kid*."

"Well, but–" Martin scratched his head. "They're protecting you, I guess," he offered uncertainly. "You're a girl, so you have to be protected."

It sounded pretty silly, but still, that was how people apparently did think, how his parents thought. Of course they'd never seen Marietta coming at them with a hairbrush. And as for that business of he got away with murder–

"You know, you're crazy," he said earnestly. "You're the one who gets away with murder. They let you say darn near anything, and I'll bet Dad's never hit you in your whole life."

"That's different," Marietta said. "They let me *say* things, but they don't let me *do* anything. And fathers don't hit girls. They deprive them of things. Have you ever noticed how many times I can't go to some girl's house, or to the movies, or to– to anything or *do* anything," she repeated, beginning to cry again.

"For Pete's sake, Marietta. You exaggerate something awful. Parents have to punish people somehow, don't they?"

"Who are you, to talk about exaggerating?" Marietta asked. But she blotted her eyes with a tissue and began to look more composed. "You're the world's champion exaggerater."

"One thing I wasn't exaggerating about— Do you remember the last time they came to anything of mine at school? They go to yours."

"Not Daddy," she pointed out. "Except the play."

"Mom has been to three things of yours this year."

"Martin, they were girl things. That's easier for a woman to go to." As Martin didn't look even faintly convinced, she went on, "Maybe it's because I'm not always in fights with people. Maybe they're embarrassed to go to school where everybody's kid practically has been—I mean, they aren't speaking to just about anyone on this street, Marty, and you know it, and it's all because of you, and you know that, too." She backed away a little, speaking in a rush.

Martin didn't move or protest. She was right of course.

"Marietta," he said suddenly, knowing he took

a chance of having her laugh at him but willing to risk it just now. "Look—wouldn't some other mother chaperone at that Fortnightly tonight? I mean, I'm getting to play my bugle tonight, and it's going real good—"

"*Well,*" Marietta said impatiently. "It's going well. Aren't you ever going to learn to speak English?"

"Okay, *well,* if that's what you want."

"It isn't what I want, it's what—"

"Okay, okay. Let's say it's going good and well. All I'm trying to tell you is, I'd like to have somebody there to hear me. I mean, I'd even like to have you," he said desperately, "if you weren't going to the Fortnightly. But don't you see—" He stopped, feeling hopeless.

Marietta looked at him narrowly for a moment, then turned and ran downstairs.

Now what? Martin wondered, slowly following. How could she work that into a complaint? He'd asked a reasonable thing, perfectly nicely, when she seemed to be in a sort of—a sort of sisterly mood. Even if she wouldn't do it, how could she beef to their mother about it?

"Mama," Marietta said. "Mama, listen to me."

Mrs. Hastings was setting the table. Martin and

Marietta were supposed to take turns at that, as well as at the dishes, but sometimes Mrs. Hastings did it in order to avoid reminding them. When she did, she always looked sort of tight-lipped. And she did, Martin realized, look tired, all right.

"Forget it, Marietta," he said. "Forget I said anything." It wasn't often he retreated from an argument, and oddly enough it didn't bother him but made him feel rather good. Sort of superior.

But again Marietta surprised him. "Mama," she said, "would you like to go to Marty's assembly tonight? I mean, instead of to the Fortnightly?"

"Well, I—" Mrs. Hastings looked at them helplessly. "I don't know. That is, of course I'd like to hear Martin play his bugle, but I'm committed to chaperoning."

"Lucy Greene's mother said she'd be glad to do it. Lucy said her mother was even sort of hurt because she hadn't been asked. You could call her."

"Yes, I suppose I could." Mrs. Hastings, staring at her daughter, then at her son, said, "What prompted this? Not that it isn't lovely to see you being nice to each other . . . but, why?"

Marietta looked the way she did when their parents asked too many questions, and Martin felt the way Marietta looked. They were being nice to each other for a change, for the moment. Why couldn't their mother let it go at that?

"I only mean," Marietta said, "that it'd kill two birds with one stone. Mrs. Greene would be pleased and so would Marty."

Things became clearer to Martin. His sister was a hero worshiper. Or maybe it'd be called a heroine worshiper. Anyway, she tried to imitate and flatter people she liked. She thought Lucy Greene was the bee's knees and Mrs. Greene even more so. Maybe because they were rich, or maybe because they were both so nice looking. But anyway, she did. If she found out that Mrs. Greene wanted to be a chaperone (*why* anyone would want to be was beyond Martin), then she would very easily sacrifice her own mother to the cause. Martin hoped his mother wouldn't figure this out, thought she probably would, and waited to see if, after all, someone was going to come to his assembly.

# CHAPTER 6

The other classes, from kindergarten up, went through what seemed to Martin interminable skits. He was pretty good about it. He didn't wriggle too much, or make faces, or—his favorite trick in assemblies—slap around at pretend insects. He sat in his chair, waiting, sometimes even watching, and as good as anyone around him.

At one point, for an amazing change, better.

The third grade was onstage, doing a wild sketch in which everybody was a number or a part of speech. The nouns and the nines were having a battle, and all the sixes and sevens and prepositions were taking sides. It was pretty exhilarating and got more so.

Jeb McCrae had brought a water pistol along with him, concealed in his jacket pocket. He had it aimed through a little slit he'd made in the seam, and in the excitement let go and hit an adverb right in the eye. The adverb let out a terrible bellow, bringing activity on the stage to a standstill. Somehow Mr. Foran, who was able to see with his eyes closed, fastened on the culprit right away, and Jeb, swearing it was all a mistake, surrendered the water pistol and just escaped being sent out in disgrace.

During all this Martin sat with a happy sense of virtue. It wasn't that he wished Jeb any particular ill. It was just so unusual, so cheery, being part of the audience to a commotion rather than the cause of it.

He turned to see his mother, to wave to her and show her how *he* was one of the good ones this time, and found her yawning widely.

After that everything went wrong. He had such a feeling of being let down at the evidence of her boredom that all the fun went out of the evening for him. He wished he'd never suggested that she come. He wished Mrs. Greene hadn't agreed to chaperone at the Fortnightly. He wished this whole dopey event would come to a close.

And just a second before he'd been so happy. Endless as they'd seemed (only because he was anxious to get to his part), he had still been enjoying what the other classes offered.

Now he sat hating it all.

The longer they took, the more bored and tired of it his mother would become, and by the time it got to the part about Martin blowing reveille, she'd probably be sound asleep.

He sat sullenly, convinced that everyone had noticed how in the entire audience his mother was the only one not interested enough to keep from yawning. Sure, kid things probably seemed like —well, like kid stuff—to grown-ups. But if their own children were involved, weren't they supposed to be interested anyway? Even if they weren't, they could pretend, couldn't they? Just to keep from embarrassing their children?

By the time the fifth grade had done its silly show about Pandora's Box, Martin was simmering. Edward Frost, in his red costume, represented one of the troubles that flew out of the box. Martin saw that his own footprint was still on one leg of the costume. He snorted. Edward and Rod and the rest couldn't have been better cast, the pests. And that Ruth Ann Silver, clambering out at the end and squealing, "I am Hope! I am the Hope of Mankind!" It was enough to make a cow sick. Hope, my foot, Martin said to himself. She looked like that fairy in the peanut butter ads. Absolutely sappy.

Finally, it was the sixth grade's turn. Martin clumped onto the stage with Otto and Jeb and the others, not talking to anybody and not caring how their skit went off. A dopey little sixth-grade thing in a dopey grammar school. Who wouldn't be bored? He was pretty bored himself, come to that. He didn't have the nerve to just walk off, but he picked up his bugle with a smirk, to indicate what he thought of it all. He wasn't going to have his mother thinking this *mattered* to him. Running his tongue over his lips, he lifted the bugle and blew.

The one thing he hadn't expected was that he would not blow right.

He'd practiced that reveille until he heard it in his sleep and could have played it in his sleep. And now? Now nothing but a gush of garbled sound, a spatter of spit, and a noise like a moose stuck in a bog.

Dumbfounded, frightened, he lowered the bugle, heard the titter of kids laughing, of people shushing them, of parents drawing their breath in. Parents always worried, all of them together, when one of the kids onstage was in trouble. In some distant part of his mind, Martin supposed it was nice of them. The front part of his mind was a shambles. What should he do? Throw the bugle down and stamp out of the auditorium? He sort of wanted to. But not completely. Wouldn't that be even more of a disgrace?

Shakily he lifted the bugle again, lowered it, stood in torment while the giggles and the shushes increased. They sounded like water coming to a boil or like stuff rattling in the bushes, snakes or like that.

"Okay, Marty," Mr. Foran said softly. "Again."

Given a direction, Martin (because he couldn't decide on his own what to do) lifted the bugle to his lips, blew, and made even a more hideous mess than before. He wanted, more than he could ever remember wanting before, to bellow, to cry, to lie down and yell and kick his feet against the floor. The way the adverb had. But, being a good deal older than the adverb, that release was denied him.

He looked painfully, through blurred eyes, toward his mother. She wasn't yawning now. She was sitting up stiff and straight, and when she caught his eye, wriggled her fingers at him and smiled, pretending everything was fine.

At the same moment Otto, behind him, whispered, "Give it another whack, Marty. You can do it."

Taking a deep breath, Martin lifted the bugle once again, arranged his lips, and blew. It wasn't good. It was a long way from this morning's beautiful, clean job. But it was a recognizable reveille, and he got through it, and then the others took over.

Martin, feeling disgraced forever, slunk to the back of the stage and wondered if a person could hold his breath long enough to die. He tried. As the recruits confused and muddled the sergeant, he tried to kill himself by suffocation. Eyes closed, he held his breath until his chest pounded and he swayed on the frail wooden chair. Then, in a rushing gasp that he hoped the dust-up on the stage would conceal, he let out a chestful of air and gratefully took in another. Funny, he'd never realized before how nice it was just to breathe. . . .

A burst of applause from the audience reached him, and he realized that the skit had ended. He got up and tried to sneak down the steps, but Mr. Foran grabbed his arm.

"Come on, Martin," he said. "You're to take a bow, too."

The rest of the boys were bowing and pushing one another and laughing at the front of the stage.

"Bow for what?" Martin asked miserably. "For practically ruining the whole thing?"

"For," said Mr. Foran, "being just about the best sport I have ever known."

It took a moment for Martin to absorb this. Then he looked up at Mr. Foran and said wonderingly, "No kidding?"

"No kidding, Marty. Now go and take your bow."

Feeling foolish, uncertain still—after all, Mr. Foran might think he'd been a good sport, and it was very nice of him, but the rest of the people—

A great big roar of applause came up from the audience as Martin reached the front of the stage. Somebody yelled bravo, and everybody was smiling and nodding at him, as if he were an astronaut or something. Martin could hardly stand it. He sniffled, smiled generally around the room, and then ran off the stage with the other guys.

All the time the girls were doing their ballet, he sat in a trance, remembering that *thunder* of applause. For him. For all the guys, but mostly for him, Martin Hastings. Even now, when he looked from the corners of his eyes, he saw people regarding him with smiles and kind expressions. As if he really was somebody. Sitting up straighter, Martin listened again in his mind to all the people clapping and calling out, for Martin Hastings.

Driving home with his mother, he said, "I guess I goofed, all right." He was waiting for her to say how he was a good sport, too, and she did. She said he had been "really magnificent."

Martin sighed contentedly. After a while he said, "I thought you were bored. I mean, you were yawning, and all."

Mrs. Hastings drove into the garage, turned off the lights, and said as they walked toward the house, "I'm not sure what you mean by *and all.* I admit I was yawning, and I'm sorry. I tried not to. But I wasn't bored, if that's what you were thinking." She stopped, patted his hand, and said, "All right, that's what you were thinking. But I wasn't. I was tired, that's all. Terribly tired. By this time of night, I just always am."

"Maybe you shouldn't have a job," he said, feeling once more that rush of sympathy he'd had in the afternoon.

"Maybe I shouldn't do a lot of things." Mrs. Hastings sighed. They went in the back door, to the kitchen. "But I do them, nevertheless. Some because I have to, like working. And some because —just because, as you would say. Like snapping at you children. Or quarreling with the neighbors."

As Martin felt quarreling with the neighbors was his fault, and he didn't want to discuss his faults just now, he said hastily, "Well, Dad gets bored. I heard him say so. At school things, I mean."

"Martin, don't complain. People are the way they are. Your father doesn't enjoy school performances, and it's too bad, but that's how it is. He's a good father, in other ways."

"Oh, sure," Martin said. "I just—"

"Try to accept people for what they are," his mother said when he hesitated. "I realize that you can't, not really, not at your age. But anyway, try. Remember it's one of the surest signs of maturity, the day you find yourself accepting people for what they are, with their good points and their bad. Would you like some cocoa?"

"Sure thing," said Martin, getting out the milk. "Only then why," he asked suddenly, "don't you and Dad? Accept *me* for what I am? Or Marietta," he added, remembering that his sister had some gripes too. Not that he thought hers were legitimate, but she *had* fixed it so his mother had been there to hear all those people applauding. It wasn't a thing he could have told them about very easily. "Why don't you?" he persisted when his mother didn't answer immediately.

"I suppose," she said at last, "because it's our job to bring you up. Children don't come into the world knowing how to behave, what the rules are. Whether you like it or not, we all have to live by rules or the world would be in constant uproar, and you'd like that even less. So, parents have to teach, and children have to learn, and I must say it isn't always easy for either party. And some people learn very hard."

She means me, Martin thought.

"Well," he said, sipping the scalding cocoa with the marshmallow floating on it, "*I* think that if people listened to their children once in a while it might be easier. For both parties," he added pointedly. He was enjoying this, having his mother to himself, talking this way, feeling safe to complain and point things out.

"You don't think your father and I listen to you?"

"Not enough," Martin said, feeling stubborn. "Like, you jump on me if I interrupt. But half the time if I don't interrupt, I don't get to say anything. Dad's always listening to Marietta or reading his paper, and you get tired. Anyway," he said, so she wouldn't have to try to think of an answer, "anyway, it's nice to *talk* about things sometimes. Even if you don't get anywhere."

"Oh, I think we've gotten somewhere," his mother said, smiling slightly.

And, at that, Martin thought perhaps they had. It crossed his mind that now would be a good time to ask about a saxophone. But he didn't ask. Because on the trail of that thought came another. To ask now might just be taking advantage. Later on, if maybe he worked in some way, or maybe they agreed to give it to him for Christmas and his birthday combined, he could ask for a second-hand saxophone. Even that would be pretty expensive. But he could get a paper route, couldn't he? Lots of guys did and paid for things themselves. Some of them, like Jeb McCrae, even saved their money toward college, a kind of foresight that was beyond Martin's understanding. But still—

Well, he would do something like that, he decided, and thereby proved, though he didn't know it, that Mr. Foran was right. In many ways he had quite a grown-up attitude.

So it was too bad that just the next morning he

got into another row with the Frosts. And all through a misunderstanding too.

For a while after he woke up, he lay in bed, thinking about last night, planning a worthy and self-sacrificing future. Then he went downstairs and fixed his own breakfast. As it was Saturday, his mother was off work and sleeping. Marietta never got up early on the weekend, and of course she'd had the old Fortnightly to exhaust her.

But Martin felt full of life and anticipation. He got three oranges from the icebox and juggled them with some success. Not much, but some. Then he squeezed them and drank the juice, savoring every tart, sweet swallow. He deliberated juggling the eggs—just two, he decided, laughing at himself because he knew he wasn't going to do it at all. Not that he *couldn't* have. But still— He fried the eggs, had toast and jam, tried a little coffee with lots of milk and found it quite tasty. Breakfast over, he debated whether to smoke one of his father's cigars, and let that temptation, also, pass from him.

He went out in the backyard and took great gulping breaths of air, thinking again what a very good thing it was, breathing.

For a moment his eye rested on the place where

Rufus's run used to be, and he felt a faint stab of the old anguish, a stirring of the old resentment. But as he wanted, today, to hold nothing against anyone, especially his parents, he looked away and forced the memory of the big puppy from his mind. Probably they thought they'd acted for the best. Yes, he was sure they did. Maybe they had been right. Martin had to admit that Rufus would be better off and happier on a farm than chained up here all day while his friend was at school.

Of course, now summer was coming, and then he would have been home all day, and then he and Rufus could have— Only he was going to be working this summer. Not all day, of course, but long enough to keep Rufe on that run too long. On the other hand if he'd still had his dog, would he have wanted to work so hard to buy a saxophone? Unable to worry out an answer to that, he wrenched his mind away from Rufus once again and looked around for something to distract him.

Glancing toward the Frosts' yard, he noticed Edward's little yellow wren house hanging in the tree. It looked cute, bobbing there in the branches. Martin wondered what Edward had made it of. It was a cylinder of some sort, but had he made the cylinder or just used an old box of some sort?

There was no one in the yard. Martin walked over cautiously and stood staring up at the wren house. It was too obscured by leaves to allow any real study.

He started up the tree to get a better look.

Just as he was reaching up carefully to examine the wren house, Edward leaned from his window and shouted, "Listen, Fatso, you get away from that birdhouse or I'll . . . I'll kill you."

Martin looked around in dismay and surprise. He'd taken for granted that Edward would still be asleep, as it was so early. Opening his mouth to explain, he got a look at Edward's face. It was filled not only with fury but with downright hate. Clearly Edward thought that Martin was climbing up there to pull the wren house down, or damage it in some way.

Furious in turn, Martin abandoned any notion of explanation. Morning, noon, and night that Frost kid was after him, like a tsetse fly. And he'd taught all his friends to make fun of Martin, too. Oh, Martin had heard him complaining to his mother about being called "Weird One" (which anyway was a lot more original than Fatso). Mrs. Frost thought her son was such an angel, but had she stopped to ask if Weird One or Fatso had come

first? She had not. How would Mrs. Frost like being called "Plump Pudding" in front of everybody?

Martin looked at his enemy. His, admittedly, smaller enemy. But a tsetse fly is smaller than a man and is still a deadly pest, it still stings and even kills people, Martin said to himself. He rested his elbow against the trunk of the tree, one cheek on his hand, and looked coldly at jibbering Edward.

"Is that a fact?" Martin drawled. "You terrify me. I mean, you actually do. I'm shaking all over." He could feel disdain and contempt drip from his voice, and he made sure Edward felt them too.

Edward disappeared, and Martin waited a moment to see what would happen now. Saturday. So Mr. Frost would be home. Sure enough, in a couple of seconds there he was, standing at the window looking angry.

"Martin," he bellowed. "Stop being such a pest. Get out of that tree this instant."

For a moment Martin considered inviting the guy to come out and make him. But then he remembered that his mother was sleeping. He thought it'd be a shame for her to wake up to a rumpus this particular morning. He started down.

"I wasn't doing anything," he said, only slightly apologetic. The Frosts really got him awfully mad, the whole bunch of them.

"Well, don't do it in our yard," Mr. Frost snapped. "And leave that birdhouse alone, do you understand?"

Never try to find out what *really* happened, Martin said to himself. Never even ask. Without further words, he dropped to the ground and walked away, sauntered away. Think they scared him, did they? In a pig's eye they scared him.

He got his bike and rode downtown to the newspaper office, where they told him to fill out an application for a job as newsboy. So he did that and then almost stopped for a frozen custard but changed his mind. Maybe if he quit eating between meals, he could take a little weight off. Mr. Foran had told him one day that if a person cut out the sweet stuff and stuck to just eating at meals and took regular exercise, the person could thin down pretty fast.

It was worth, probably, a try.

And when he got the newspaper route, which the people at the paper were almost sure he would because guys were always quitting, he'd walk it, not bike. If, along with that, he played volleyball or baseball in the afternoon (if the guys would let him, and maybe Otto could talk them into it), why he ought to be thin as a stick in no time.

With this inspiriting vision before him, he rode home to find his mother and sister flying around the house packing suitcases.

"What gives?" he asked his mother, watching her closely to see signs of a visit from the Frosts. Apparently they'd decided to give it a miss this time, too, because she smiled at him brightly and said that their father had telephoned from Cedar Rapids.

"He says he's finished his calls there earlier than he expected, so if I'll drive all of us up, we can take my car and go on a little trip. Perhaps even to Canada. Won't that be fun?"

"Sure thing," Martin said happily. "Can you get off work?"

"Oh, yes. I telephoned the office and explained that as this was my children's spring vacation, I'd like a week, and they said fine. So . . . so it's fine. Go and start packing, Marty. We'll leave right after lunch."

Martin bounded up the stairs, forgetting to tell them about his practically certain job.

Canada, huh? He'd always wanted to see Canada. Or any other place, for that matter. But Canada was a good start.

All in all, Saturday was proving an excellent day.

# CHAPTER 7

There was a strange man at the Frost house. He'd come while the Hastings family were taking their trip through Canada.

Not only the man, but a dog, a collie type just about the age of Rufus when Martin lost him, had come too. Martin was not interested, just at first, in the man, who looked like any other grown-up, except maybe a little tanner for this time of year.

He was desperately interested in the dog.

It seemed so enormously, so bitterly, so entirely not fair for Edward Frost, who had—his very own parents admitted it—no sense of responsibility (and no sense of anything else, so far as Martin was concerned) to wind up with a dog.

"It isn't his dog," Mr. Hastings had pointed out to Martin. "It's his uncle's."

This distinction seemed to Martin stupid. He knew, even if no one else did, that that dog was going to be Edward's. Maybe the uncle didn't think so, maybe Edward's parents were certain that the dog would be there only as long as the uncle was. Maybe Edward himself didn't know. But Martin *knew* that that collie, Argess, was next door to stay. She wasn't Rufus, by a long shot, but a lovely dog still, and the sight of her opened an old wound in Martin's heart.

The trip to Canada had been great, just great. The Hastings family had enjoyed the sights, the driving, the motels. They had been pleased with the vacation and with, for a change, one another. Even Martin and Marietta had gotten along "like brother and sister," Mrs. Hastings had said. After a moment Martin saw what she meant. Instead of like cat and dog.

He had come back still full of determination. He was going to get a job, study hard, be nice, be good, be friendly with everybody. To, as his mother had asked him, accept people (that included parents) as they were.

It all proved easier to plan than to carry out.

For a couple of weeks he did go at his school work harder than ever before in his life. He had the time, certainly, because nobody asked him to play ball, and after all he could not bring himself to beg Otto to shove a wedge in for him. A person's pride was more important even than baseball, or even than getting thin. So he came home early each day and (partly to avoid the sight of Edward with that dog) went immediately to his room and bored into his books with the concentration of a caterpillar chewing through oak leaves. He grabbed no one's hat, beat up on nobody, and didn't sass a single adult. He didn't have a piece of cake or a bar of candy. He practiced a lot on his bugle, in order one day to deserve a saxophone. Without talking about it, he tried his very best to live up to all his own promises to himself. Yet, almost every day when he came home from school, old Mr. Eckman, from the security of his porch, shook a thin white fist and called something about, "You young rascal, why don't you pick on someone your own size?" Since he now wasn't picking on anyone of any size and furthermore hadn't talked rudely to old Prune Face since last fall, this seemed pretty unfair. But Martin, eyes on the future, would stomp past saying nothing.

There is an old proverb which goes, "Get a reputation for rising early, and you can sleep till noon."

It seems to work in reverse, too. Get a reputation as a sluggard, and rising at dawn won't alter it. Or, anyway, not for a long time.

Martin decided that being a reasonable, responsible person was bringing no rewards. Then he decided it was bringing one. This was a feeling he had within himself. He found he liked doing his work in a concentrated way. It became more interesting. It was a relief, really, not to be fighting all the time, not to be the one held up before the class as a terrible example. He liked the way it was around home. Now that he and Marietta weren't squabbling all the time, now that some of the neighbors were speaking to her again, his mother wasn't so stern and jumpy. And while his father never offered to throw a ball with him in the evening and didn't yet seem to care much how Martin's day had gone, he at least wasn't forever saying Pipe down. Now and then he even listened to some story with his coffee, instead of diving behind a newspaper the second dessert was finished. And Martin wasn't doing anything to earn himself a spanking.

The people at the newspaper office told him he could have a route beginning the day after school let out for the summer, and telling the family about this was one of Martin's happiest moments. He had, with great forbearance, withheld all mention of the job until he actually got it.

"Why, darling," said his mother, "how simply marvelous of you. How enterprising. How smart. How—" She ran out of words and just smiled. In a flush of joy Martin mentally sacrificed the saxophone and offered aloud to put all his earnings toward the family budget.

"Now, Marty," his mother said, "you know that won't be necessary. I think you are showing great independence of spirit, and I'm proud of you. But you keep what you earn. Perhaps you could save some of it toward something you might want someday that we couldn't afford."

Martin almost told her about the saxophone then but decided to wait until he'd really saved something toward its purchase.

His father claimed to be overwhelmed at the news. Martin felt that this was overdoing it, but he was in no mood to quibble, so he took his father's praise too, with that feeling of warmth and comfort that words of praise always brought him.

"But I thought," Mr. Hastings said, "that you wanted to go to camp this year?"

"No," said Martin. "I mean, I wanted to go this

year last year, but now I guess Marietta can go again. I'm going to be too busy."

Marietta was so delighted that she offered to take Martin's turn at the dishes every night until she left. She actually did a couple of times.

When he remembered how much he'd wanted, last year, to go to camp, Martin was sort of surprised at himself. But then, a lot of things had changed since then. It occurred to him that possibly just getting older had something to do with it. Maybe, after all, some problems were solved just by a person's getting older. This was an encouraging idea, and he was glad he'd had it.

In spite of Edward's having the dog, in spite of how slowly news of the "new Martin Hastings" was getting around, things in general seemed to Martin dandy, just dandy.

He should have known it was all too good to last.

One day toward dismissal time, a day of warmth and fragrance outside that made everyone in the stuffy classroom restless and a little out of sorts, Martin fell into a dream of such intensity that he failed to hear Mr. Foran calling upon him for the answer. Lost in a year far removed from this classroom and these people, he failed, apparently, to hear him about four times. . . .

It was the year when the name Martin Hastings would be on everyone's lips. Martin Hastings, the greatest saxophone on earth, taking Russia by storm on his good will tour. The Great Russian himself was saying, "*Martin Hastings, you and your music have done what all the summit conferences and negotiations failed to do, you have bridged the gap between our peoples, and from now on—*"

"Martin Hastings! Stand up this instant!"

*Martin Hastings, stand and receive this Cross of Honor—*

"Martin, do I have to come down there and pull you from your seat?"

"Huh?"

Martin struggled out of his dream to find the entire class in a state of suppressed laughter and Mr. Foran, far from laughter, drilling into his eyes with eyes that spoke of trouble.

" 'Scuse me," Martin mumbled. "What did you say? I mean, Mr. Foran? Did you ask me something?"

Jeb McCrae swallowed a yelp and earned a fierce frown from the front of the room. Mr. Foran, however, was concentrating so hard on Martin that he let Jeb off easily.

"Martin, are you being deliberately obstructive?"

"No," Martin said. "No, sir. I was . . . I mean, just thinking."

"Not, obviously, about what I am attempting to teach during the present hour."

"No," Martin said without thinking. The rest of the kids could hardly keep still, and Martin hurried on, "I mean, sure. Yes, I was. I was thinking about it so hard that I got carried away."

"Carried away scarcely expresses it," said Mr. Foran. Apparently the languor of the day had gotten to him, too, and made him, like the rest of them, edgy. "Well," he went on bitingly, "now that you're back within hailing distance, possibly you'll deign to answer the question?"

Martin hated sarcasm. More than an outright scolding, he hated from a teacher words that pretended to be patient but really invited amusement from the other kids. Good intentions vanishing in a second (or perhaps they'd been evaporating from lack of recognition), he fixed Mr. Foran with one of his looks and drawled, "Well, I just guess you'll have to repeat the question. I mean, so it makes sense."

Otto, at the desk behind, gasped. Even for Martin this was going pretty far. Mr. Foran stood dumbfounded a moment, and then said flatly, "Remain after class, Martin. I'll attempt to . . . make sense to you at that time."

Martin swallowed nervously. His moment of rashness past, he was left with the usual residue of rashness—agitation and remorse. Now what? All the good work of the past few weeks gone up in smoke, just like that, just in a few words. He doubted that even Mr. Foran, usually pretty easygoing, pretty understanding in spite of a quick temper, would take that kind of insolence without going to, at the very least, the principal. And maybe his parents, too. And how would his father react? Badly, that was how. His father wasn't going to like it the least little bit.

Oh, *crums,* Martin said to himself angrily. He wondered if grown-ups had any notion, any remembrance at all, of how hard it was trying to live up to their standards of what was good.

When the bell rang and Martin remained in his seat, Mr. Foran waited until all the other pupils were gone, and then he looked at Martin with an expression of great weariness. He said,

"Martin, go home. I've changed my mind. I don't want to try to make sense to you, because I doubt if anyone could. Just go."

This upset Martin more than being kept in and lectured could have. For a moment he considered demanding to be punished, but a look at Mr. Foran told him that he wouldn't be listened to. Then he thought of apologizing, or trying to, even though apologizing was a very difficult thing for him to do. But Mr. Foran was putting his papers together with a look on his face that seemed to forbid any more talk.

Martin got heavily to his feet and left with a feeling that the end of the world had come, that there was no point in trying to be nice or good or praiseworthy, because something like this would always happen.

On the way home Mike Toomy, another buddy of Edward's, shouted, "Hey, you sausage, whyn't you go fry yourself?"

Martin, only half hearing, kept walking.

But when he got near his house, as he passed Edward's, there was Edward's bike, parked half-way into the Hastings' driveway. The sight of it filled Martin with rage. He'd told Edward again and again to park his dopey bike out of the way of the drive, so that when Mr. Hastings came home at night he wouldn't have to leave his car and move it. Shoving the bicycle over, Martin pushed it into the Frosts' driveway and stamped indoors, where he ate a pint of ice cream and almost a whole box of gingersnaps. Call him a sausage, would they? Okay, then . . . he'd eat like a sausage. As he said this to himself it struck him sort of funny, and for just a moment a smile tugged at his lips before he recalled how little he had to smile at.

He went up and tried to blow on his bugle, made a mess of that, tried to do his homework and couldn't concentrate. Finally he just stared out of his window. In the Frosts' backyard Edward and his uncle were sitting on the grass together, talking, looking up now and then at the wren house. Argess was lying next to Edward, her head on his leg.

Watching them, so peaceful, so friendly, with a dog like Argess theirs to pet and call to and be with, Martin was almost engulfed in pain. There was that terrible sensation of half strangling to keep back childish tears, and another feeling—that of being someone completely alone. It reminded him of the way he felt whenever he went in a place where people already were—a class-

room, dancing school, even a public place like a drugstore. It always seemed to him that the people who were already there sort of owned the place, belonged there, and that he was an outsider pushing his way in and not welcomed. After a while, of course, he'd get over it, and when other people came in, it was as if he belonged and they didn't. But he hated that feeling of being outside, unwanted, not *part*.

All the kids were crazy about Edward's Uncle Josh. He was a hobo. A gentleman of the road, Mr. Frost called him. Martin's father called him an adventurer. "In the best sense of the word," Mr. Hastings had added, sounding a little jealous of Uncle Josh's way of life. Mr. Eckman had been heard to call him a bum. But, no matter what you called him, he was a person free to stay or go, free to do as he wished. Probably the most enviable man who had ever come to town, most of the boys thought. They hung around him a lot, and he told them stories about his travels. He let kids do anything at all, never interfering or suggesting that they were being silly or childish or that they were running risks. As much unlike a parent as a grown-up could possibly be.

Well, I'm not crazy about him, Martin said to

himself, staring down at the three friendly beings on the grass, the boy, the man, the dog. I think he's sort of . . . of *mean,* he told himself defiantly. He has this way of looking at you as if you weren't there at all.

Martin had, one time, tried to engage Uncle Josh in a conversation across the hedge. But the man hadn't answered or even turned his way. He'd looked as if he were asleep, but his eyelids had flickered a little at the sound of Martin's voice, so he'd heard all right. He just hadn't wanted to be bothered. At the time Martin had said to himself that maybe Uncle Josh was day-dreaming and didn't want to come out of it. This was a thing Martin understood, because he did it so much himself. But now . . . now he could only remember that one more person had snubbed him. Coming from a man with a reputation for liking kids, for being friendly with them, made it worse. Made a person, he said to himself again, feel not *part.*

You couldn't trust them, not any of them.

He turned away from the window, picked up his bugle, ran down a scale, put it aside and decided to go out. He'd bike downtown and look in store windows at second-hand saxophones.

*Martin Hastings, the greatest saxophone on—*

Well, the feeling wouldn't come. That was a silly dream, he knew. But still, it was sort of fun prowling around downtown, looking at the window displays of the two music stores.

He went downstairs, started for his bike, then stopped in surprise. There was a note fastened to it with scotch tape, a note written in large red letters. Martin glanced around, saw Edward sitting on his porch, hugging his knees and apparently waiting for something to happen. Suspiciously Martin ripped the note from his handlebars and read it.

MY BIKE CAN LICK YOUR BIKE, it said.

Martin blinked, read it again, then looked over at Edward, who was now sitting up at attention. In spite of himself Martin laughed. It really was funny. MY BIKE CAN LICK YOUR BIKE.

Edward was watching him carefully, a sort of bright attentiveness about him, and just for a second Martin had a hope that possibly they could, here and now, finish the feud. This funny note offered them a way out. In truth Martin would welcome one. He tried to think of something funny and agreeable but not *too* friendly to say. Edward was not to get the notion that he was in any way chicken. Well, for a start, he could just say it was pretty funny. Since it was.

He looked up from the note just as Argess, sitting at Edward's side, leaned over and licked the boy's ear. Watching, a passion of protest and envy rose in Martin, blotting out friendly impulses. Rufus, the only living being that had ever accepted him just as he was, was gone. Rufus used to lick *his* ear in just that way, but now Edward was the one with a dog. And Martin was once again in trouble all around.

It was more than Martin could bear. He curled his lip scornfully and said, "Pretty funny. I bet you never thought of it yourself, Weird One."

Edward hesitated. "Not exactly," he said. "I mean, my uncle and I—"

"Oh, yeah," said Martin. "Your uncle. I heard about him. The bum."

"He's a traveler," Edward said hotly.

"Bum is how I heard it."

Then something happened that Martin never in the world would have expected. Weird One, gamy little Edward Frost who always ran because he was outweighed, ran this time straight for Martin, who was so surprised he forgot for a second to defend himself. He received a punch in the eye and one on his head before he started to fight back, and even then it was no pushover. Edward was like a wild man, throwing his fists about in erratic punches. One of them, landing in Martin's stomach, almost took his breath away.

His superior strength asserted itself shortly, and Martin got Edward on his back. Grabbing the smaller boy's head, he began to pound it up and down on the lawn. Blind with anger and humiliation and the accumulated frustrations of the day, he probably banged the head harder than he'd meant to. He was just about to ease up, get up, when a cannonball of fur and teeth descended upon him.

Growling, snarling, scratching, Argess got a grip on Martin's shirt and pulled till he heard it rip.

Letting out a bellow of fright, Martin released Edward and tried to defend himself from the dog.

Then all of a sudden it seemed that everyone on the block was there. His own mother and Edward's, screaming and threatening, shrieking at Uncle Josh to make them stop. Uncle Josh, commanding Argess to let go, pulling the boys apart. And a circle of buzzing neighbors.

"Young bully, never does pick on anyone his own size," Martin heard.

He wanted to say, Mind your own business, Prune Face, but could hardly get his breath at all and had none to spare for rudeness. He glared at Edward, who glared back triumphantly.

"What's going *on* here?" Mrs. Frost said. "Edward, what happened?"

"What happened," Mrs. Hastings said tensely, "is that you have a vicious dog that attacked my son and I'm going to call the police, that's what I'm going to do."

Martin looked down at Argess, who was panting and staring from one person to another. For a moment her eyes caught Martin's, and he could see in them nothing but the lovely brown eyes of Rufus. She looked friendly, not angry at all. She'd just done for Edward what Rufus would have done for Martin.

"The dog had nothing to do with it," Martin said. "It's this kid, this—" He gestured toward Edward, his tormentor.

"This child, who's half your size," Mrs. Frost said. She moved forward a few steps, and Martin's mother moved to meet her, and for a second it really seemed that they were going to get into a fight, too.

Suddenly Uncle Josh burst out laughing. "Haven't any of you people ever seen a couple of boys fight before? It's a natural—"

"Natural?" Mrs. Frost yelled, almost crying. "This—this *bully* never fought a boy his size in his life. He goes for smaller children always—"

His face scratched and swollen, a feeling of doom pressing down on him, Martin felt the blood rise to his face. It was true, of course. Not the way it sounded, not as bad as it sounded, and there were reasons they didn't understand. But all the explanations in the world weren't going to help. What she said was true.

Edward, looking upset, said, "Mom—" But nobody listened.

"I'd hardly call it an uneven fight," Mrs. Hastings said to Mrs. Frost, "when a mad dog is introduced on your child's side. I'm going to have the police on you, that's what I'm going to do," she said again.

"Mother!" Martin shouted. But nobody heard him either. Suddenly he couldn't stand any of it one second longer. He bolted for his house, and when he got inside could hardly climb the stairs. His legs were shaking too much.

When his mother came in, she led him up to the bathroom and washed his face with cold water.

"Mom—" he began, his face muffled in the washcloth. "You see—"

But she said, "Don't talk about it, Martin. Just . . . try to forget." For a moment she pulled him against her. It was the first second of peace Martin had known all day.

In the evening Mr. Frost came over to complain and as usual got nowhere. Mr. Hastings said they'd all be lucky if the police weren't brought into it, and Mr. Frost said not to threaten him, he wouldn't put up with it, so Mr. Hastings told him to go fry an egg and Mr. Frost told *him* to go boil his head.

Mr. Frost went away looking dissatisfied, and that seemed to be the end of it.

At first Martin couldn't believe his father wasn't going to spank, scold, or punish him in any way. But he didn't. He said, "I wish you wouldn't get into fights, Martin. Try some other way of settling your grievances. There *are* other ways, you know."

Speechless, Martin stared at his father.

"It's tough, isn't it," said Mr. Hastings, "trying

to live down a reputation as a bully? Bad to get it in the first place, and worse to get rid of it."

Never would Martin have believed that his father would understand this. Still he couldn't say a word.

"I know you've been trying hard these past weeks," Mr. Hastings went on. "And I guess something happened today that was too much for you." He lifted a silencing hand. "I don't want to hear about it, Marty. Whatever it is, you'll have to take care of it yourself. I only want to say that you've been making a good try, and your mother and I know it."

Going to sleep that night, Martin decided that he'd apologize to Mr. Foran in the morning. Apologizing was a hard thing to do but not impossible. He'd do it. To Mr. Foran. He'd choke before he'd apologize to the Frosts for anything.

He thought a little about Argess and sighed for his lost rambunctious puppy. But mostly he thought about his father. He wasn't the sort you read about. The kind who was a pal to his son. But a pretty good father, anyway, if you halfway cooperated with him. Maybe even the pal-type fathers lost their tempers once in a while and preferred to read the newspapers when their children wanted to talk. Maybe that was just what happened to people when they grew up.

He was sure he'd never understand grown-ups. Not now, or soon, or even in that distant, not at all believable time when he himself became one. Thinking of that, of actually and forever being grown up, with no chance of going back, he burrowed into the pillow and was glad that there were still so many years between now and then. Maybe getting older solved some problems, but getting too old made you an adult, and that was a condition he had no wish to be in.

# CHAPTER 8

One day Mr. Foran cut the history lesson short and began to talk to the class about their future in junior high school.

"I believe you'll find it very interesting," he said, and then made one of his little jokes. "Should be a welcome change, anyway, not to have the same teacher all day long."

The class smiled, and a few made friendly protests. Martin found, all at once and to his astonishment, that he was going to miss Mr. Foran. It wasn't a thing you could say out loud, in front of everybody, but there it was . . . a fact.

"Try, as much as you can," Mr. Foran was saying, "to take part in extracurricular activities. Join the various clubs. Language and science clubs and the athletic teams. Run for office in your Student Government." His eyes traveled the room, rested on Martin. "I have one particular suggestion, which is that our very inventive friend Martin should try out for the school paper or magazine. Pity to waste those colorful narratives on forgetful ears."

Martin decided on the spot to try out for both. He could see his name, in bold print, leading all the other names. *Martin Hastings, Editor-in-Chief*. He sighed with dreamy satisfaction.

Martin lied less and less lately. But he made a distinction between lies—which were told to escape punishment—and exaggerations—which were, well, just exaggerations. Tales and fables, told to make life more interesting. But he'd learned that not all people made this distinction. So probably writing his stories out and *calling* them stories would be one way to satisfy everybody.

*Martin Hastings, Editor-in-Chief*. It sounded great, no question about it.

Martin had made, recently, the surprising discovery that admitting a thing, anything, made it somehow easier to cope with. When, for instance, people kidded him about his weight, or even when they were not kidding but unkind, he no longer blew up and said angry things in return. He told them that it wasn't easy to get that fat and was even harder to get thin again. That stopped them, all right.

Toward June he realized that it had been ages since he'd called people dopes or bat brains or dumbbells. And people in his class were calling him Marty. (Otto and Jeb, with kindly patronization, called him "son.") He hadn't heard a Blimpo or Fatso from anyone in his class for ages.

One day after school Jeb stopped him and said, "Say, son, would you like to lend your literary talents and your inventive mind to a baseball game this aft?"

Martin looked happily at Jeb and said he'd like that fine.

So it went. A step at a time, Martin made his way out of the bully's desert.

On the other hand, his reputation was still dying a hard death among older people, and younger. Mrs. Sonberg accepted him, but warily. Mr. Eckman no longer called unpleasant remarks from his porch, but he fixed Martin with a pale cold eye every afternoon when Martin walked past toward home. And although Martin hadn't made a move toward Edward Frost in ages—hadn't even talked to him—Edward and his friends still hollered,

"Where are you off to, Plump Pudding, a date with the fat lady?" when they thought they could safely outrun him.

Exercising his new-found forbearance, Martin wondered when the heck they were going to notice that he wasn't chasing them now, or grabbing their hats, or calling them names. When they were going to notice and admit that he'd outgrown them. When, for Pete's sake, were they going to observe his loss of weight?

Some fifth-grade boys, shooting past on their bikes one afternoon when Martin was walking, stopped to taunt him. One shouted, "Better watch your step, Blimpo. Edward's building a trap for fat boys, and when you fall in he's going to beat you up again, like last time!"

"Beat me up!" Martin scoffed. "Hah!" It was too silly even to get angry about. He kept walking.

"Beat you up is how we heard it."

"Beat me up!" Martin repeated, and felt his temper slipping. "Look, if that shrimp beat me up, I'll march on him with every guy in the sixth grade, to avenge my honor!" With this extravagant and nonsensical threat he turned and proceeded toward home in a dignified manner.

Late the next day, on an errand for his mother

at the supermarket, Martin ran into Otto, there on an errand for his mother.

"Hey, did you hear?" Otto said, looking up from frowning concentration on his list.

"Hear what?" said Martin, who as usual had lost his list and was trying hard to remember what he was here for. "Hear what?" he said again when Otto appeared to go into a trance.

Otto thrust the piece of paper at him. "Does this say soup or soap?" he asked.

Martin looked. "It says onion right in front of it. Do you use onion soap at your house?"

"Hey, that's right. It does," said Otto, brightening.

"Did I hear what?" Martin said again, trailing along.

"About Rod Graham and Edward Frost?"

"No," Martin said, feeling an unaccountable queasiness. There was something about that expression "Did you hear?" that usually meant you were going to hear something not good. "What about them?"

"They ran away."

"Ran away?" Martin said. "Ran away from what?"

"From home, from home," Otto said. "How

many cans of soup do you think I ought to get?"

"For the luva mud, Otto, how should I know? How many cans of soup do you eat in your house?"

"You don't eat soup, you drink it."

"That depends on how thick it is. Some soup, like bean soup, for instance, you practically have to use a knife and fork–"

"I'll get three," Otto decided.

"Otto, will you stop yakking and tell me why those guys ran away?"

"How should I know?"

"How do you even know they did?"

"Because Mrs. Graham telephoned my mother, that's how. She's having a fit. They didn't show up at school this morning, and this afternoon a cop–policeman–phoned from some town up north–he phoned Mrs. Frost because the Grahams were out somewhere–and said he had two runaways in jail there.

"In jail!"

"Yeah. Isn't that the ant's pants? Mrs. Frost left ages ago to pick them up." Otto shook his head and pushed on toward the checker.

"Run away, huh?" said Martin. By now he'd left his wagon and was just strolling along, keeping

Otto company. "Wouldn't have thought they'd have the nerve," he said half enviously.

"I wouldn't have thought they'd be so dumb," Otto said. "It's a kid's trick. Besides, where can you run to these days that you won't get caught? Unless"— he grinned a little —"unless they headed for the open sea, like you were going to. Maybe they made contact with your sea-going uncle in Gloucester, eh, old son?"

Martin lifted his shoulders slightly. "I've got this very active imagination, see?"

"Boy, do you ever," Otto said, but he sounded admiring.

Martin missed the admiration, because he was feeling a little uncomfortable. There was that dumb threat he'd made to Edward's friends. They couldn't have taken that seriously, could they? How could anybody with any brains at all take a thing like that seriously? No—he was just being jumpy. It was so dumb there was no chance of its being true.

By the time he got home, he'd forgotten Edward, Rod, the threat, and anything connected with them. He'd also forgotten to buy any groceries.

Still—for once it didn't matter. His parents were out to dinner at some friend's house, and Marietta was staying overnight with Lucy Greene. He'd shop tomorrow and not lose the list or anything.

Now he pottered around happily getting dinner for himself. Some chopped beef, salad, peas and carrots, half a melon, and some dietetic cookies his mother had got for him that he didn't think much of but ate anyway, because they took up space in his stomach.

Still, it was funny how once you'd put stuff like cake and pie and frozen custard out of your life, it got easier to do without them as time went on. Or maybe it was easier because he weighed himself every week (the doctor who put him on the diet said not to do it every day as that could be sort of discouraging) and every week he weighed less than he had the week before. A vision of himself, tough and thin as Otto and Jeb themselves, went before him like a carrot before a donkey, and he pursued the vision while ice cream and candy streamed past and away, forgotten.

Almost forgotten.

He was just getting to the melon and cookies, and thinking about the job he was going to start next week, when the doorbell rang. He answered, to find Mr. Frost on the porch.

Despite all the Frost-Hastings trouble, Martin had always rather liked Mr. Frost. When he'd been younger he'd even wished that Mr. Frost could have been his father instead of Edward's. But his heart sank, seeing him now. Mr. Frost looked big and stern and determined. He looked terribly serious and very upset. And somehow he was going to connect all this to Martin, of that there could be no doubt at all.

"What's the matter, Mr. Frost?" Martin said edgily. "Something wrong?" He knew darn well what was wrong, but he wasn't going to say. Those blasted kids—getting in trouble. That was all going to be blamed on *him,* was it?

"May I come in, Martin?"

"Sure, sure. Come on." Nervously leading the way to the living room, Martin said again, "Something wrong?"

"Martin, I believe you know what's wrong," the man said, sitting down, leaning forward a little.

"No, I don't. Honest, Mr. Frost. I don't know what you're talking about."

"You don't know that Edward and Rod ran away this morning?"

Martin started another denial, changed his mind

and said, "Look, Mr. Frost, there's some sort of mix-up, see?"

"I know there's a rumor that you threatened to line up the sixth-grade boys and lay for Edward after school today. . . ."

"Well—" Martin began, and stopped, considering how to put his case.

"Let me say now," Mr. Frost went on, "that I do not believe your threat was entirely responsible for this—escapade. But it contributed, do you see?"

Martin licked his lips. "Well—" he said again and stopped again. How could he put it so that this man would understand? "—You see, some guys stopped me yesterday and said Edward was building a trap for fat boys, to catch me in—" Mr. Frost drew his brows down in annoyance, though at whom Martin couldn't be sure. "In the first place," he hurried on, "I'm not so fat any more. I'm on a diet. Only they don't notice. And in the second place, I haven't even looked at Edward or Rod, not since the day—since—"

"I know the day you refer to," Mr. Frost said. He sounded gentler now.

"Well, then—" Martin spread his hands, as if in conclusion.

"You mean, you said *nothing* to the boys yesterday? They made it up?"

"Oh, crums," Martin breathed. He took a moment for organization, plunged on. "Look, Mr. Frost. It's like this—I haven't been paying any attention to *them*, but they go right on paying attention to *me*. Like calling me names, and all. Well, I've been trying to—to rise above them—" He detected a flicker of sympathy in Mr. Frost's eyes, and went on, encouraged. "So there you are. I've been leaving them along, and I'm not so fat, but they don't notice," he repeated. "I've been waiting and waiting for them to. Not," he added proudly, "to be friends, or anything like that. Just so they'll drop that Fatso business."

"It's hard, living down a bad reputation," said Mr. Frost.

"That's what my father told me. But he said after a while even a good reputation catches up with a person."

He saw that Mr. Frost looked surprised for a second. Which, said Martin to himself, is just another part of the stuff that it's hard to live down. Everybody on the block knew that Martin and his father didn't get along, so they'd never see that they did. Or, anyway, that they were getting along a lot better than they used to. But he was darned if he was going to explain anything about his parents to the father of that pest Edward. "Anyway," he continued, "those guys said that Edward had beat me up that day. But that's not so. Argess beat me, I guess. But, holy cow, I can't have people saying someone Edward's size beat me up, can I?"

"I can't see that it's any worse than someone your size beating Edward."

Martin reddened. "I'm not," he said sulkily. "Not any more. That's what I'm *telling* you. But they said that, so I just made up a dumb threat. To scare them off, like. I mean, Mr. Frost, who'd believe me? Who'd ever think I could *get* all the sixth-grade guys to do something for me? Crums . . . half of them only started *talking* to me fifteen minutes ago. I was exaggerating, see? I do that a lot."

"Yes, I can see that you do," Mr. Frost said with a smile. "Martin," he continued, "there's something I've observed about you, and that is that you're an excellent sport in many ways. The night of the assembly, when you played the bugle solo—" He stopped. "Am I bringing up something too painful?"

"Oh, no," said Martin, who'd flushed a little, but

not in embarrassment. He'd been remembering again the heady sound of that applause. "No, that's okay. Sir, I mean." He waited to hear more about how he was a good sport.

"Well, I appeal to that sportsmanship in you. Will you continue to—to ignore the boys? Edward and Rod and their friends? Ignore them, and behave as you've been doing, and in time they'll see that you certainly have risen above them. Or anyway above the situation. What I'm trying to say is, they'll probably continue to be little pests for quite a while, but if you can keep your temper—"

"Oh, I can do that," Martin said grandly. "I look upon them as mosquitoes." He realized that he was speaking to one of the mosquitoes' fathers and said hastily, "I mean to say—"

"I know what you mean to say," Mr. Frost put in, smiling again. "Well, I'll have a talk with Edward, and who knows, one day you might be friends."

Martin thought this quite unlikely, but decided it would be smarter not to say so. "*Did* they run away, Mr. Frost? I mean, holy cow, how could they run away because of such a . . . such a dumb threat?"

"They didn't precisely run away," Mr. Frost

explained. "The policeman who called said they'd been accidentally locked in an empty refrigerator car and carried off. They had played hookey, all right, and gone down to the freight yards."

Martin whistled.

"Exactly," said Mr. Frost. "We're so frighteningly fortunate that the thing didn't end in—" He wouldn't say what was in his mind.

Still, it was perfectly clear to Martin. Those silly kids could have been shoved to a siding in their refrigerator car and not discovered until—until too late. He found that he was glad this hadn't happened.

"We've been very fortunate," Mr. Frost repeated. "Mrs. Frost left this afternoon right after she heard from the police, and the boys should be back pretty soon." He got up to leave. "Look, Martin," he said, "it wasn't just what you said that sent them off. That was only part of it. Rod had been in trouble with his father—"

*You see,* said Martin's face. *I'm not the only one.* But he listened, not speaking.

"And Edward—" Mr. Frost sighed heavily. "Edward, you know, is crazy about Argess."

"Who wouldn't be?" Martin said simply.

"Well, what's happened is this . . . we woke up

this morning to find Josh, my brother-in-law, gone. And the dog with him. I guess that was Edward's main reason for playing hookey. He felt betrayed. What happened after that was just a chain of circumstances."

"You mean he went and took Argess?" Martin yelled. "Why, that's—that's—" He clamped his mouth shut.

It was horrible. It was, in a way, almost like losing Rufus again. Not the same to him, of course, but the same sort of treachery on the part of grown-ups, who did what they pleased and didn't care how kids felt at all. A surge of the old bitterness welled in his heart, and he looked at Mr. Frost with dislike for what he represented—the world of adults.

"I make no defense for Josh," Mr. Frost said. "Someday, when you're grown, Martin, you'll find that things can't always be as simple as children would like them to be. The human being is extremely complicated, with the good and the bad all mixed up."

Martin stared at the floor. Take people as they are, his mother had asked him. Take them with their good points and their bad. Even if the people took other people's dogs away?

"My brother-in-law is what he is," Mr. Frost said. "And a good man in many, many ways. But the fact remains that he comes and goes without much reference to other people's feelings."

The famous Uncle Josh, Martin thought. With his stories, his easygoing manner, his faraway eyes. Idol of all the kids who knew him. But not a person anyone could rely on. At least, he thought to himself, my parents *warned* me. They gave me plenty of chances. And at least they put my dog where he'd be happy. Argess, he knew, would not be happy away from Edward. That was just how it was. Maybe because she was a female dog and gentler than the wild-hearted Rufus, not so crazy about running around and being free. Unlike Rufus, she wouldn't have been alone most of the day. She obeyed. She didn't bark too much. Yes, he felt sure Argess would be happier with Edward than with Uncle Josh. Martin admitted this and felt a surge of fierce pride in his own untamable Rufus.

"You know, Argess won't like this," he said to Mr. Frost.

"You're a wise boy," the man said. "She didn't. She came back. Josh came with her, to be sure she found her way. He says she kept turning around and starting back all the time he was trying to go forward. Forward to what, I don't know," Mr. Frost concluded, mostly to himself.

Martin, his mind on Argess and not on Uncle Josh, nodded sadly. From time to time he'd hoped that Rufus, like dogs in books and newspaper stories, would leave that farm and make his way back over the miles to his young owner. But the last time Martin had asked, Mr. Hastings had said that Rufus was still on the farm, and seemed to be enjoying it thoroughly. He'd become a good cow dog, with the entire herd under his control. Proud of his dog, and hurt by him, Martin made up his mind not to ask any more. He guessed if he could accept people as they were, he could do no less for Rufus.

"So Argess is back," was all he said.

"Yes, she's back. Martin," Mr. Frost said, turning at the front door, "maybe after things quiet down, after you and Edward get to understand each other, you could share her."

Martin looked at the man kindly. He meant well, and it wasn't his fault that he was too old to remember that boys do not share dogs. He saw Mr. Frost out, as his mother and father saw their guests, and then he went in to get the melon and the dietetic cookies.

Someday he'd have a dog again, a dog of his own. But meanwhile there were plenty of things to occupy his time, take up his attention. He wouldn't be able to take care of a dog now, anyway, and handle his newspaper route, play ball with the guys, practice his bugle, do his schoolwork well when he began junior high. A person could stretch himself just so far.

But someday he'd have a dog. It wouldn't be Rufus. There would never be another Rufus. But he'd love the next dog, too, in another way, for himself.

Getting out his bugle, he blew a honey-smooth reveille, just for fun. Now that the newspaper job was a sure thing, he intended to tell his parents about how he wanted to save for a saxophone. Then, at Christmas maybe, they'd get him a secondhand one for Christmas and his birthday combined, along with what he'd saved himself. A saxophone was a darned expensive instrument. He could almost feel it, heavy and gleaming, in his hands. He could feel his lips readying themselves, could feel his indrawn breath, the lift of his head. . . .

*Martin Hastings, the greatest saxophone on earth.*

On earth? Martin laughed a little. Who knew, if things kept going the way they were, guys tooling around the world in an hour and out toward the moon in no time at all—and there was no reason why things *shouldn't* keep on that way—why, maybe one day . . .

*Martin Hastings, the sweetest sax on the moon—*

## *About the Author*

MARY STOLZ, one of today's most distinguished and versatile writers, is the author of more than 40 books that have been enjoyed by millions of young readers. Among her many honors was the nomination for the 1975 National Book Award for her novel THE EDGE OF NEXT YEAR, and she has had several of her books, including A WONDERFUL, TERRIBLE TIME; A DOG ON BARKHAM STREET; THE NOONDAY FRIENDS; and CAT IN THE MIRROR chosen as ALA Notable Children's Books. She is also the recipient of the George G. Stone Center for Children's Books 1982 Recognition of Merit Award honoring the entire body of her work.

Born in Boston and educated at the Birch Wathen School and Columbia University in New York City, Mary Stolz now lives with her husband, Dr. Thomas C. Jaleski, on the Gulf coast of Florida.